The Demon's Den

THE HARDY BOYS® MYSTERY STORIES

THE DEMON'S DEN

Franklin W. Dixon

Illustrated by Paul Frame

WANDERER BOOKS
Published by Simon & Schuster, Inc., New York

Copyright © 1984 by Simon & Schuster, Inc.
All rights reserved
including the right of reproduction
in whole or in part in any form
Published by WANDERER BOOKS
A Division of Simon & Schuster, Inc.
Simon & Schuster Building
1230 Avenue of the Americas
New York, New York 10020

Manufactured in the United States of America
10 9 8 7 6 5 4 3 2
10 9 8 7 6 5 4 3   pbk

THE HARDY BOYS, WANDERER and colophon
are registered trademarks of
Simon & Schuster, Inc.

Library of Congress Cataloging in Publication Data

Dixon, Franklin W.
The Demon's Den.

(The Hardy Boys mystery stories)
Summary: The Hardy boys, vacationing in Vermont, offer
to help the police locate a missing camper and find themselves involved with a doomsday cult, a deadly strain of
bacteria, and possibly the devil.
[1. Mystery and detective stories] I. Frame, Paul,
1913–   II. Title.   III. Series: Dixon, Franklin W.
Hardy boys mystery stories.
PZ7.D644De   1983   [Fic]   84-3616
ISBN 0-671-49724-3
ISBN 0-671-62622-1 (pbk.)

Contents

1 *The Missing Camper*

VVVRRROOOOOOOOOOMMMM!!!

"Hang on!" Joe yelled above the roar of the engine as it kicked into full throttle. The green speedboat shot over the surface of Lake Ketchumken, its bow bouncing high in the air!

At the sudden surge of power, Chet Morton dropped his fishing pole and tumbled head over heels out of his seat, landing with a crash on his tackle box.

"Hey!" the chubby youth complained. "Are you trying to kill me?"

Grinning sheepishly, seventeen-year-old Joe Hardy flipped the throttle switch down a third.

"Sorry, Chet. I didn't know this baby had so much juice. Are you okay?"

Chet checked his body for bruises as he climbed back on his seat. "Most of me's still here," he grumbled. "But next time you try stunt-driving, give a little warning first!"

Joe's older brother Frank, who had grabbed the gunwale at the unexpected burst of speed, agreed wholeheartedly. "Why the hurry, anyway?" he asked.

"I saw two police cars over there," Joe replied, pointing ahead. "So I thought we should take a look."

Frank scanned the far shore of the lake. Three cherry-red flashing lights were just visible through the early-morning fog that drifted over the water's surface. They seemed to be coming from a cluster of lakeside cottages.

The dark-haired young detective pulled a pair of high-powered binoculars from a duffel bag and studied the scene up close. Several small cabins lined the water's edge, and behind them was a lodge with the words CAMP KETCHUMKEN painted in huge letters on its roof. Three squad cars were parked outside, their top lights flashing.

"You're right, Joe! It seems there's a problem," Frank called from the bow. "Take her in!"

Chet moaned. "Oh, no. We haven't been here a day yet and already you two have your noses in someone else's business! I don't have time for this. I've got some serious fishing to do!"

Frank smiled. "You'll get plenty of time to catch Old Sam," he said with a wink. "That is, if he really exists."

It was the first morning of the boys' vacation. Their friend Biff Hooper had invited them to spend two weeks at his parents' cottage in Vermont, and the trio had leapt at the chance to get away from the hot streets of Bayport. Frank, Joe, and Chet had set out right after breakfast to scout around the lake in the Hoopers' green skiff.

Lake Ketchumken was full of nooks and coves worthy of exploration. And Chet wanted to hook Old Sam, a legendary giant bass reputed to lurk at the bottom of the lake. Many people had tried to catch the famous giant fish, but all had failed.

Joe nosed the flat boat to shore in front of the cabins.

"Old Sam can't wait all day," Chet said, as his companions hopped from the boat. "I'll pick you guys up in an hour, when this nonsense is out of your systems."

As he motored back out on the lake, he had no idea that the Hardy boys had just stepped into one of the biggest mysteries they would ever tackle.

The campgrounds swarmed with young boys, many of whom were gathered near the police cars. Several state troopers leaned on the cars' hoods.

"Hi!" Joe addressed the officers. "What happened?"

A tall sergeant with bushy brown eyebrows glanced at the visitors. "A kid is missing," he replied tersely. "Who are you?"

"I'm Joe Hardy, and this is my brother Frank. We're amateur detectives and we thought we might be able to help."

"Oh, you did, eh?" The sergeant chuckled. "Well, that's mighty decent of you boys, but I think we can handle this all by ourselves."

"I wouldn't turn down an offer from these fellows if I were you," a husky man spoke up from inside one of the squad cars. Then he opened the door and stepped out. He was short and muscular, and had curly dark hair. "These youngsters are the sons of Fenton Hardy, one of the top private detectives in the country," he went on, and smiled at the embarrassed

10

sergeant. "And from what I've heard, they've already made quite a name for themselves in our business."

"Thanks." Frank blushed at the praise. "We're used to being kidded because of our age. That's half the reason we're successful. Nobody takes us seriously until it's too late."

The husky man shook the boys' hands. "I'm Lieutenant Henderson, chief detective for the Vermont State Police. I've admired your father's work for years. Please forgive Sergeant Biddle here."

The bushy-browed officer also shook the Hardys' hands, then the lieutenant began leading them around the camp.

"Let me fill you in," he said. "We received a call from the director about a half hour ago. He told us that one of his campers—a boy named George—was out in the woods with a friend last night. But when the friend woke up this morning, George was gone."

"Maybe he went off to collect firewood or something and got lost," Joe chimed in.

"That's what we think happened. But the director is worried."

Lieutenant Henderson opened the door to the lodge and gestured for the Hardys to enter. "I'm

11

going to talk to him now. Would you like to come along?"

"Sure," Frank replied eagerly.

The director of Camp Ketchumken was seated behind his desk in the office. He was a big, Nordic-looking man, with smooth features and straight blond hair. In front of the desk stood a boy with thick glasses and freckles. He seemed to be about ten years old.

"Larry, these are the Hardy brothers," Lieutenant Henderson said. "Frank, Joe, this is Director Larry Smith."

Smith hesitated as he held out his hand. "What did you bring them in here for?" he asked.

"They happened to be in the area. And since they're well-known detectives, I thought they might be of help."

Somehow the director seemed displeased with the Hardys' presence, even though he tried not to show it. "Let me get right to the point," he began, leaning forward in his chair. "Do you know the abandoned barn at Needle Point Cove?"

"Yes," Henderson replied. "It's just up the shoreline a ways. Do you think George went there?"

"I don't know," the director replied. "But I worry about that crazy cult who uses it. They call themselves Apocalypse and believe that the world is about to end. I hear they perform strange rituals to ward off doomsday."

"I've heard about them," the detective said with a sigh. "But it seems they're just a bunch of harmless crazies."

Smith slammed his fist on his desk and shot out of his chair. His face was red with anger. "Harmless?" he snapped. "Do you mean you have to wait until they actually hurt an innocent boy before you can put a stop to their madness? I knew something like this would happen, ever since those doomers took over the barn! It's less than two miles from my place and I've forbidden my campers to go near it. But a kid like George gets curious—and whammo!"

"Aren't you jumping to conclusions?" Henderson asked evenly. "There's no evidence to suggest—"

"Yes, there is!" Smith cried. Then he focused on the boy in front of him and softened his tone. "Ken, tell the policeman what George said to you last night before you went to sleep."

Ken looked at the floor and spoke in a timid voice. "He said he wanted to check out the barn

13

and see what was going on. But I was too scared to go with him. George called me a chicken. Then we went to bed. But I guess he got up and went there after I fell asleep."

"*Is that* enough evidence for you?" the director said hotly. "George must've gone to watch the cult in the middle of the night, and when they caught him spying on them, well . . . who knows what they did!"

"Now, there's no reason to think he's been hurt," Henderson declared. "But you're right. We must investigate the barn immediately."

"Have you contacted George's parents?" Frank asked.

"No," Smith said, eyeing the young sleuth with distaste. "I don't want to worry them just yet. Once this gets out, Camp Ketchumken's reputation will be ruined!"

Ten minutes later, Mr. Smith, the troopers, and the Hardy boys marched through the forest along the lake. The ground was matted with a soft bed of pine needles and the sky was all but blocked out by high branches, enabling the group to approach the old barn without being noticed. It stood in the center of a small clearing, its roof full of holes and part of its wooden frame rotted away.

"All right, men, surround the place," Hender-

son ordered. "If anyone's in there, we don't want him getting away."

The officers fanned out while the Hardys, the camp director, and Henderson headed straight for the dilapidated building. They knocked on the door. There was no answer. They opened the door and peered inside, their eyes adjusting to the dim interior light.

"Wow!" Joe breathed. "What a strange place!"

The walls were painted in a hellish mural of monsters, flames, and grotesque, winged serpents. Rows of wax candles encircled the dusty floor, and in the very center of it all stood a makeshift stone altar.

"It's a fire hazard if nothing else," the short, muscular police detective remarked, peering at the candles.

The dirt floor was covered with footprints, and Frank stooped down to inspect them. "These are fairly fresh," he announced. "The cult must've had a meeting here less than a day ago."

Joe walked slowly to the stone altar and examined it in fascination. Engraved on its surface was the cult's ominous emblem—a picture of the earth in flames. As he looked around the rough stone, he suddenly gasped. "Those footprints aren't the only things around here. Look what I just found!"

2 A Weird Cult

Joe held up a T-shirt with the words CAMP KETCHUMKEN on it.

"I knew it!" the director screamed. "It's George's shirt. These crazies got him! He may not even be alive!"

"We don't know for sure this shirt belongs to George," Lieutenant Henderson cautioned. "Matter of fact, it looks much too large for a twelve-year-old."

"George is very big for his age," Larry Smith informed him. "His dad's a football player and his mother's a former Olympic speed skater. Both parents are top athletes, and George is the national swimming champion in his age group.

Even though he's only twelve, he's six feet tall already and weighs at least one hundred and sixty pounds!"

The officer nodded grimly. "I'll have my men look around for any other signs of foul play," he said. "Just try to relax, Mr. Smith."

"Relax? You must be kidding!"

The detective turned to Frank and Joe. "Why don't you and Mr. Smith go back to camp and see if you can find anything there? Meanwhile, we'll scour this area with a fine-tooth comb."

"Sure," Frank said. "Will you call us if you have any news?"

"Certainly. Tell me where you can be reached."

Frank gave Henderson the phone number of the Hooper cottage, then he, Joe, and Director Smith hiked back through the woods.

"Why were George and Ken camping out last night?" Joe asked, as they made their way among the tall pines.

"Oh, it's something all the campers do once or twice during the summer. It gives them a chance to use the woodsman's skills we teach them at the camp—cooking over a fire, building a shelter from pine branches, setting up their tents, and so on."

"Do you mind if we take a look at the spot

where the boys spent the night?" Frank inquired.

Smith shrugged. "Go ahead. But I don't have time to take you there. Maybe Ken can go with you."

Once back at Camp Ketchumken, the Hardys looked for the boy, but it turned out he was away with a group of youngsters and a counselor exploring nearby caves.

"Try later," Smith said. "They should be back in about three hours. Now I'd better go and call George's parents. I wish I didn't have to, but I don't think I can postpone it any longer." With that, he disappeared into his office.

Frank and Joe went to the dock, where Chet was waiting in the skiff.

"What's going on?" their friend demanded.

"A boy disappeared while camping with another kid in the woods last night," Frank said, and told Chet the whole story.

Chet shuddered when he heard about the Apocalypse cult. "Maybe they make human sacrifices at that altar!" he blurted out.

"I doubt it," Frank said. "There wasn't a trace of blood anywhere. And according to Lieutenant Henderson, the group is considered quite harmless. I have this funny feeling—"

"That Larry Smith was a bit too eager to pin

the guilt on the cultists!" Joe finished his brother's thought. "He wasn't too pleased that we appeared on the scene, and not at all cooperative when we asked if we could investigate George and Ken's campsite. You'd think if he were really interested in finding the boy, he'd welcome all the help he could get!"

"I see we're on the same wavelength!" Frank grinned. He turned to Chet. "Do me a favor and drop us off about half a mile from camp. I'd like to double back while Smith thinks we're gone."

Chet shrugged. "Whatever you say."

"How did you do?" Joe asked his friend as they were chugging along the shoreline. "Any nibbles from Old Sam?"

"Not yet," Chet replied. "But I hooked a couple of sunnies. See?"

Two small sunfish, not more than six inches long, were swimming about in a pail Chet had balanced between the ribbing in the outboard's frame.

"Those aren't enough to tempt a cat!" Joe teased. "I want Old Sam on my plate for supper tonight, not a scrawny little sunfish."

"Just hold on to your old rod and reel!" Chet countered. "I haven't begun to fight. Anyway, even if I do catch Old Sam, I'm not planning to serve him up. I'm going to have him stuffed and mounted."

Joe guffawed. "Oh, really? I thought eating was number one on your priority list."

"I prefer hamburgers," Chet defended himself. "I'm only fishing for the sport of it."

Frank, who'd been busy studying the contour of the lakeshore, nodded toward a clump of trees. "Okay, we've gone far enough, Chet. You can drop us off here."

Once the Hardys were on land again, they circled through the woods back to Camp Ketchumken. They scouted around the grounds, keeping out of sight of the youngsters and counselors, eavesdropping on conversations and watching for anything unusual. However, after a couple of hours they came up with nothing helpful.

Suddenly they saw Ken tramping down a dirt path. Joe blew a sharp whistle to attract the boy's attention.

"Hi," the young camper said when they stepped out from behind a clump of bushes. "What are you guys hiding for? Did you find out what happened to George?"

"Not yet," Frank replied. "But we're working on it. Can you show us where you two were camping last night?"

"Sure," Ken offered. "Follow me." He led the young detectives up a hill and over a mass of rocks to where the ground leveled off. The overnight shelter was a simple lean-to made of pine bows and a stripped branch lashed between two trees. In front of the lean-to were the remains of a campfire.

The sleuths made a quick search of the area. The needle-covered ground showed no footprints at all, but there was something inside the lean-to, where the needles had been cleared away, that caught Frank's interest.

"Hey, Ken!" he called to the young camper. "Do you know what made this mark?"

Ken stooped to inspect a smooth gouge in the dirt that appeared to have been made from a spear. "No." The camper shook his head. "But that's just about where George was lying."

Frank eyed the young boy keenly. "Are you sure you didn't see or hear anything strange around here late last night?"

Again, Ken shook his head. "No. I was sleeping."

Frank knew that if there had been a struggle, Ken would have woken up. Stumped, he sat crosslegged on the ground and gazed at the smooth round gouge in the dirt. He felt it somehow tied in with George's disappearance. But how?

"Do you think George is big enough to defend himself if someone attacked him?" he asked Ken.

"You bet! He's really huge and strong. Did you know that his dad is Mark Watley, the forward for the Boston Beacons? They were in the playoffs last year."

"Now we're getting somewhere!" Joe snapped his fingers. "Longlegs Watley earns a million dollars a year. That makes his son a perfect target for kidnapping!"

"I wonder why Mr. Smith didn't tell us," Frank said. "He did mention George's dad was a football player, but he didn't say which one."

"You mean someone's holding George for ransom?" Ken asked excitedly.

"We don't know yet. But it's a possibility. Look, don't tell Mr. Smith about any of this, okay? He doesn't want us around, but with your help we may be able to solve this mystery!" Frank said.

Ken's eyes were shining. "You really think so?"

"Why not?" Joe said. "But remember, no talking about the case until it's solved."

"Don't worry, you can count on me!" the boy promised.

The group hiked back to the camp, where the Hardys found Lieutenant Henderson in the director's office, but Larry Smith was not there.

"We think George may have been kidnapped," Frank told the detective.

"It's quite likely," Henderson replied. "Larry called the Watleys; they're on their way up now. I've staked out the old barn. The first cult member who shows up is going to be brought in for questioning."

"Mr. Smith never told us that George was Mark Watley's son," Frank said. "I wonder why."

Henderson shrugged. "He's very upset about this whole thing, as you can understand. He probably didn't think of it." With that, he got up and walked to the door. "See you later."

Frank and Joe continued wandering about the camp. "We have to find out all we can about Smith," Frank said. "I think he's a likely suspect in this case."

Joe nodded. "Maybe Dad can—" He was interrupted by a muffled shout. "Shh!" he said. "Did you hear that?"

"Yes. It sounded like someone calling our name," Frank replied.

Then they heard the voice again. "Hardys!" a man called under his breath. "Come here!"

The sleuths looked around to see where the voice had come from, until their eyes settled on a lone figure standing fifty yards deep in the woods. The figure wore a long black cloak and its head was draped in a black hood!

"What in the world . . . ?" Frank breathed.

3 A Mysterious Figure

"Come here!" the black-hooded man uttered a second time.

"It may be a trap," Frank warned, scanning the forest for other hooded figures. "Be careful!"

The brothers slowly approached the mysterious man, who retreated farther into the woods, suddenly disappearing behind a mossy rock embankment. When they came to the spot where he had been standing, Joe noticed a piece of paper stuck on a tree.

"Look at this!" he exlaimed, ripping it off. "That guy left us a note!"

26

Frank leaned over his younger brother's shoulder, and together they read the message.

HARDYS. COME TO NEEDLE POINT AT MIDNIGHT. DO NOT BRING POLICE. DO NOT TELL ANYONE, OR YOU WILL NEVER KNOW WHAT HAPPENED TO THE BOY.

The note wasn't signed, but it bore the same emblem that had been carved on top of the stone altar—a picture of the earth in flames.

"He was a member of the Apocalypse cult," Frank remarked, looking puzzled. "I wonder what they want with us."

Joe shook his head. "I don't know. But I'm afraid the only way we'll find out is by playing along."

"That's true," Frank agreed as he folded the note and shoved it in his trousers pocket. "But it might be dangerous. Let's take the boat there so we can make a quick exit if we have to."

Needle Point, the boys had learned earlier, was the tip of the nearby narrow spit of land that formed Needle Point Cove.

With renewed hopes for a clue to George's whereabouts, Frank and Joe trudged back to Camp Ketchumken. Once there, they found George's parents in the office.

"Is there any news of our son?" Mrs. Watley asked in a trembling voice after introductions were made. She was over six feet tall and very strong-looking, with a pretty face and short, curly hair. Her green, oval-shaped eyes were edged with tears.

"Not yet," Frank replied. He resisted the urge to tell her about the mysterious note, however. It had been clear—DO NOT TELL ANYONE, OR YOU WILL NEVER KNOW WHAT HAPPENED TO THE BOY. George's mother was too distraught to be trusted with the secret, and to go against the cult's demands might cost them their only chance of finding the missing camper or put his life in further danger.

Joe jotted down a number on a piece of paper and handed it to Mr. Watley. "Please contact us if you hear anything," he said.

"You mean if I receive a ransom note?" The football star sighed, wearily easing his huge form out of the chair behind Smith's desk.

"Yes, sir," Joe responded sadly. "We're really sorry about all this, Mr. Watley."

Frank and Joe left the office and marched around the lake to the Hoopers' cottage. It was now late afternoon and they hadn't seen their friend Biff since breakfast.

"Hi, guys!" he called out from the front porch when he saw the Hardys emerge from the pine forest. Biff was a blond, lanky boy with an ambling gait. He'd spent the day working out on a punching bag he'd constructed on the porch to get himself in shape for the football season.

"Where've you been all day?" he asked, giving the bag one last swipe. "Chet told me you've already gotten yourselves tangled up in a new mystery at the camp across the lake. Something about a missing kid."

Frank and Joe sat down on the porch steps and recounted the day's events. Biff's father, blond and lean like his son, joined them and listened to the tale.

"We'd like to borrow your skiff again tonight," Frank said when he'd finished. "We also have to make a long-distance call to Bayport, if it's okay."

"No problem." Mr. Hooper smiled. Then his face became serious. "But I want you boys to be very careful. That cult sounds weird, all right. I wouldn't want to have to call *your* mother with the same news Mrs. Watley got today."

"Don't worry. We'll watch out." Joe promised, remembering the forlorn look on George's mother's face.

29

The Hardys went into the cottage and Frank dialed Sam Radley's number on the phone. Sam was a private detective who often helped his father on his cases. He was especially good at researching financial data on companies and other business ventures.

"You said the name of this place was Camp Ketchumken?" Sam's voice crackled over the line.

"Yes, and the director's name is Larry Smith," Frank replied. "See what you can dig up on him, will you, Sam?"

"Will do. I'll get back to you as soon as I have the information."

Frank put the receiver down and glanced at his brother. "If we get a solid lead tonight, maybe the case will be solved by the time we hear from Sam."

The sun was starting to set over the lake when Chet beached the Hoopers' green motorboat in front of the cottage. Aside from a nasty sunburn, all he'd caught were a few more sunfish and a couple of perch. The perch were big enough to eat, so the boys cleaned and broiled them for dinner.

"Any sign of Old Sam yet?" Mr. Hooper asked as they ate around the kitchen table.

Chet shook his head. "No. But I think I know

where he hangs out. It's a spot up at the north end of the lake where the water's really deep. No other fish seem to be around that spot, and I bet it's Old Sam's territory. He scares them all away."

Frank grinned. "You'll be a good match for each other, Chet."

After cleaning up the dishes, Frank and Joe waited until shortly before midnight. Then they boarded the skiff and made their way in the pale moonlight toward Needle Point. Once there, they circled the point twice, scanning the dark trees for any sign of the cultists. There was none.

"Take her in," Frank said. "We'll have to check further on land."

Joe throttled the outboard and eased it in to shore, where they fastened its painter to a bush limb. Then they cautiously crept through the woods to the tip of the point. Still, they saw nothing and heard no more than the gentle rustle of the night wind and the constant chirping of crickets.

"I wonder . . ."

Just then, a cloaked figure stepped from behind a tree, its face concealed by a hood.

"I'm glad you came," a man said in an eerie, hollow tone.

Joe took a step forward, hoping to unmask

31

him, but about thirty more hooded men suddenly appeared from among the dense pines! Instantly, the boys were surrounded.

Frank and Joe felt the blood drain from their faces.

"We aren't going to harm you," the leader droned. "On the contrary, we want to hire your services. We heard that you are amateur detectives and are already investigating this case."

Frank breathed an inaudible sigh of relief. "You belong to the Apocalypse cult, don't you?" he asked faintly.

"Yes."

"Hire us for what?" Joe blurted. "What's this all about? Where's George?"

"If George is the missing boy from Camp Ketchumken, we want to hire you to find him," the man declared calmly.

"But in the note you said you knew what happened to him," the blond youth protested.

"We do. But we don't know where he is."

Frank looked at the hooded cultists, who encircled them like dark statues of doom. "I think you'd better explain," he said evenly. "Who are you? Why did you want to meet us out here? What do you know about George?"

"We are Apocalypse," the veiled stranger declared, raising his cloaked arms like wings. "It is our mission to prevent the Devil from taking this world and consuming it in flames. To achieve this, we must live in darkness and secrecy. The end is close. The Devil is nearly upon us. We are the only ones who can stop him, because we are invisible. And because we are invisible, we are strong. We fight the Devil as he fights us, fire with fire."

"Does that mean kidnapping innocent boys?" Joe demanded hotly. "George's T-shirt was found at your barn!"

The cult leader gasped. "We did not kidnap anyone. All we have learned is that a camper is missing and that the police believe we were behind his disappearance. The T-shirt must have been put there purposely to make people believe we took the boy. The Devil is a crafty creature."

"Where do you come from? Who are you?" Frank asked.

"We are ordinary people like you—businessmen, housewives, students, craftsmen. We came from Canada to help because we know the end is near and we must prevent it."

"Tell us what you think happened to George," Joe queried.

"The Devil has him!" the leader exclaimed, his voice rising in dramatic crescendo. "When we hold rituals, some of our members are chosen to stand watch in the woods in case someone tries to invade our meeting. Last night, one of the guards saw a large man on his way through the forest. He was prodding a young boy along in front of him with a pitchfork, the same kind of pitchfork the Devil's helpers use to do his dirty work."

"Did he get a good look at this . . . Devil's helper?" Frank asked.

"It was too dark. And our watchman didn't dare try to stop one of the Devil's own agents."

"What does this supposed pitchfork look like?" Frank inquired, remembering the spear-like mark they had found at George and Ken's overnight campsite.

"It has a long handle and a small head," the cultist said, "with short, sharp prongs."

"Why didn't you inform the police about this right away?" Joe asked, still skeptical of the tale.

"The police would never believe us! They think we're crazy!"

"And you thought we *would* believe you?"

"We knew you wouldn't arrest us and throw us in jail! If we went to the police, they'd lock us

34

up! That's why we want to hire you boys to prove the Devil did it and not us. If we're arrested, our identities will be unveiled and our powers lost. Then the earth will soon be devoured in a great ball of fire!"

"Where do you believe this Devil is?" Frank asked seriously.

The black-hooded cult leader made a grand, sweeping gesture with his arm. "Satan inhabits the land far to the north, where few people dare to go. He is busy building an army of men the size of trees with which he will conquer the earth. It is said he lives far up a river that runs both ways."

"Can you be more specific than that?"

The man shrugged. "We know no more. The Devil keeps himself well hidden while he builds his army. You must go there and find him. Then you will also find the boy."

"We'll do our best to find George," Frank said as he turned to leave. "And you won't need to hire us. If you're innocent, you have nothing to worry about."

"The Devil took the boy!" the man insisted. "You must find him soon, or the world will perish!"

The Hardy boys returned to their boat and

sped back across the lake to the Hoopers' cottage. They could hardly wait to tell Chet and Biff about their strange encounter. But when they arrived, Chet greeted them with pressing news of his own. "Your father called," the chubby boy said. "He wants you to phone him right away. It's urgent!"

4 *Midnight Meeting*

The brothers ran into the cottage and dialed their number in Bayport. Fenton Hardy answered immediately.

"I want you to do me a big favor tomorrow," he said. "Sorry to call so late, but I was afraid I'd miss you in the morning."

"Yes, Dad?" Frank asked.

"Listen carefully. The National Institute of Health in Washington, D.C. has just hired me to track down a team of scientists. About ten years ago, it seems, these people were working on a special government project involving genetic engineering. But the project was discontinued because it was considered too dangerous. Now the National Institute of Health wants me to locate all members of the team."

"Why?" Frank asked. "And how do we fit in?"

"During their project," Mr. Hardy replied, "the scientists were exposed to a new bacteria strain they had developed, a deadly strain that was immune to drugs. If the bacteria had spread to the general public, it could have wiped out an entire population. At the time, the men were quarantined until NIH was sure they hadn't absorbed the deadly germ. Then they were released. Now, research indicates that the scientists *could* be carrying the bacteria within their bodies—without knowing it."

Frank whistled. "You mean they could still set off a major epidemic?"

"That's right," Mr. Hardy replied. "Now, I've located all but one of these men. The last one, whose name is Randolph Rhee, was seen by one of his associates some time ago. This associate is Jeffrey Peters, who is now with the Vermont Biological Research Center. I talked to him over the phone, but he said he knew nothing of Rhee's whereabouts."

"So you want us to visit Jeffrey Peters and see

if we can find out more?" Frank asked.

"I'd really appreciate it. He may remember something else if you meet him and pick his brain a little."

"Will do, Dad," Frank promised, and jotted down the address of the biological research center.

"Call me around suppertime," Mr. Hardy added. "I'll be in New York all day."

"Okay." Frank quickly filled his father in on their own adventure, then hung up the phone. When he had related the request to Joe, the blond boy looked puzzled.

"It seems strange that after ten years it should be so urgent to find these guys," Joe said. "Besides, genetic engineering is the process of splicing the genes of living organisms together to produce new life forms. How do deadly bacteria get into this?"

Frank shrugged. "Search me. All I know is we have to talk to Jeffrey Peters."

The Hardys went out to the porch again and told Chet and Biff about their midnight rendezvous at Needle Point. Their friends listened wide-eyed to the story about the black-hooded cultists who believed that an agent of the Devil had abducted George.

"They sound crazy, all right," Biff remarked.

"In some ways, you're right," Frank agreed. "But in spite of their wild story, I think there's an element of truth to it."

Suddenly Joe chuckled. "You know what's funny about that story?" he asked. "It reminds me of Old Sam. Chet said he'd tracked the legendary bass to a spot on the north end of the lake, where other fish were afraid to go. Tonight the cult leader said he thought the Devil lived in the north country, where no man dared go, and where he was building an army of giants."

"Now don't go comparing me to that crazy Apocalypse cult!" Chet protested. "I *know* Old Sam's out there, for sure."

"I think it's time for you to hit the hay," Joe teased his friend. "You're so tired you're acting delirious."

"And remember to wear a hat from now on," Biff piped in playfully. "I think you got a little too much sun today."

The next morning, Frank and Joe were up early for a breakfast of pancakes and sausages. Then they made an appointment to see Jeffrey Peters in the afternoon.

"We still have to find out how that T-shirt got in the barn," Joe commented. "If the doomers didn't kidnap George, someone must have planted it there."

Just then the phone rang. Joe picked it up and heard Sam Radley's voice.

"I dug up some interesting info on Camp Ketchumken and its director, Larry Smith," Sam reported. "It looks as if the camp is in desperate financial straits and is in danger of going under. The Internal Revenue Service is also on Smith's back for a heavy tax liability. The man is up against the wall financially."

"That's all we needed to know, Sam," Joe said, beaming. "Thanks a lot."

He hung up the receiver and snapped his fingers. "That clinches it. From now on, we stick to Smith like glue!"

Instead of using the skiff to get across the lake, the brothers drove their yellow sedan around to the camp. Lieutenant Henderson was outside the lodge with George's parents. They had received no ransom note, and the police still had no clue to the missing camper's whereabouts.

"Where's Mr. Smith?" Frank inquired casually, not yet prepared to divulge his suspicions or tell Henderson about the midnight meeting.

"He took a bunch of campers on a field trip to a lumberjack contest," the detective replied.

"Guess he wanted to keep the kids' minds off what happened to George."

"Lumberjack contest? That sounds like fun!" the dark-haired boy exclaimed, faking enthusiasm. "Where is it?"

"Up at Green Mountain Park, not far from here on Route Twenty-nine. They hold one every year. Lumberjacks from all over compete in log rolling, ax throwing, sawing, pole climbing—you name it."

"I'd like to see that, wouldn't you?" Frank asked his brother, winking secretively.

"Sounds great! Why not?" Joe responded.

Leaving Henderson and the Watleys befuddled, the Hardys jumped back in their car and drove out to Route 29, a two-lane highway that wound up into northern Vermont. Following a road map, they soon arrived at Green Mountain Park. Over its entrance a bright banner welcomed them to the ANNUAL LUMBERJACK CONTEST.

"I see the campers," Joe said as they crossed the parking lot. "But I don't see Smith."

"Neither do I," Frank agreed.

A throng of people sat on a grassy hillside, waiting for an event to begin. In the center of the contest area was a small pond for the log-

42

rolling competition, and next to it was a mound of logs, a row of sawhorses, and a tall, wooden pole for the tree-climbing event.

The sleuths went to join the campers. Two counselors were with the children, but the director was nowhere in sight.

"Where's Mr. Smith?" Joe asked one of the counselors, a gangly boy about his age.

"He's entered the contest," the boy replied. "He does it every year. Right now he's getting ready in the lumberjacks' quarters. It's that red building over there."

A thought flashed into Frank's head. "Come on," he whispered to Joe. "I have a hunch."

The Hardys marched to the red, barrackslike building behind the contest area, where they were stopped at the door by a rugged, uniformed guard.

"Sorry," he told them. "Only the participants are allowed in here."

"Where do we sign up?" Joe asked impulsively.

"At the booth around the corner. But it'll cost you ten bucks for each event you enter, so don't waste your money unless you're real good. We've got some of the best lumberjacks in the U.S. and Canada here today!"

Joe pulled out his wallet as he jogged around the red barracks to the booth, but Frank stopped him short.

"Hold on, Joe," he cautioned. "When Smith sees we've entered the contest, he's bound to become suspicious. Let's call Chet and Biff. He doesn't know them."

"All right," Joe agreed, "but they'd better get here fast. The show is about to start."

The boys called the Hoopers' cottage from a public phone booth near the parking lot. Luckily, Biff and Chet were still there and agreed to the plan. By the time they wheeled into Green Mountain Park in Biff's jeep, though, the first contest was already under way. All they could enter was the log-rolling event. After they had paid their fee, they went to the loggers' quarters.

"Make sure the place is empty," Frank told Biff. "It should be, by now. Then open the back door."

"Sure." The spunky boy nodded.

Biff and Chet showed their tickets to the guard and went into the red building. Bunks were lined up along the interior wall for the lumberjacks who had come long distances and were staying overnight. Boots, hats, ax-sharpening stones, cans of oil, duffel bags, and other gear cluttered the area around them.

"This is a far cry from the smell of the great outdoors!" Chet commented sarcastically, getting a whiff of the woodsmen's quarters.

"Easy, Chet," Biff warned his friend. "When was the last time *you* ever worked up a good, honest sweat?" Chet took a swipe at him, but missed.

As Frank had predicted, all the men had left the building when the contest had begun, so Chet and Biff hurried to the back door and let in the Hardys. The young detectives scanned the room quickly until their eyes settled on what they'd hoped to find.

On the wall, just below a mounted moose head, was an old log jammer that the park service staff had hung on display. Once used for negotiating logs down rivers, it had a long wooden shaft with a steel hook for snagging.

"I think we've just found ourselves one Devil's pitchfork!" Joe exclaimed. "And I bet it's also what made that groove in the dirt at George's campsite."

Frank took the old log jammer off its mount and studied it carefully. Traces of fresh dirt coated the spearlike steel tip!

5 An Embarrassing Contest

"We'd better call Henderson," Joe said.

Frank nodded, and was about to put the old logging tool back on the wall when a gruff male voice rang out from behind them.

"What are you doing here?"

The boys, who had been too absorbed with the log jammer to notice the man come in, spun around to face him. He was one of the lumberjacks—a burly fellow with greasy black hair and a full beard. His eyes were closely set and piercing under his beetling brows.

"We're in the competition," Chet replied. "We have a right to be here."

The logger glared at them. Biff and Chet had

dressed for the contest, wearing their oldest jeans and T-shirts. But the Hardys were in crisp khaki slacks and clean sport shirts.

"What about you two?" the burly man grunted, revealing a thick French accent. "Do not you tell me that you go in contest with those clothes!"

"No," Frank said evenly. "We just came to watch our friends."

The young detective figured that the lumberjack was one of a tough breed of French-Canadian woodsmen, whose ancestors had roamed the wilderness of North America long before the first settlers had crossed the continent. They were said to have the cunning and instinct of wolves, and from the stranger's bushy beard, leathery skin, and fierce eyes, Frank could tell that he wasn't to be taken lightly.

"Then you get on out of here," the man ordered. "And I will take the other two with me."

Chet gulped and looked pleadingly at the Hardys, but a glance from Frank told him to do as the stranger said. Following the French-Canadian, Chet and Biff marched out to the contest area, while the Hardys went straight to the public phone and called Lt. Henderson at Camp Ketchumken.

"Sounds like you're on to something," the de-

47

tective said. "I see why you haven't told me before, but from now on, I want you to keep me informed. Understand?"

"We will," Frank promised. "By the way, have you rounded up any of the Apocalypse cult yet?"

"We have three of them at the station right now. They're giving us the same crazy story about the Devil they told you last night. I'll have to hold them until they come up with a better one."

Before hanging up, Frank and Lt. Henderson agreed to tell nobody but George's parents about their suspicions. If the camp director *was* involved with the kidnapping, he was more likely to lead them to George if he felt safe.

"Now, let's see how poor Biff and Chet are doing," Frank said quickly when he was off the phone.

The brothers jogged up the grassy hill that overlooked the contest area. The log-sawing competition was in full swing at this point and the crowd was cheering wildly. Two lumberjacks were gripping a double-handled saw, and, with dust flying, they ripped through the timber with lightning speed. When they were finished, their time was marked down and the next team stepped up to try and beat it.

"And now," a loudspeaker blared, "we'll see the skill of the director of Camp Ketchumken, Mr. Larry Smith from Vermont, and his partner for this event, from the Canadian province of Saskatchewan, Mr. Pierre Lafoote!"

"Uh-oh." Joe frowned. "It's him."

Joining Smith at the cutting block was the burly lumberjack who'd just thrown the boys out of the barracks.

"I sure hope he didn't tell Smith about seeing us," Frank murmured. "It could cause a lot of trouble."

"Especially since you were holding that log jammer when he caught us," Joe added. "If Smith found out about *that,* he'll know we're barking up the right tree!"

The referee readied his stopwatch, raised the starting gun into the air, and fired. The men cut into the log with rapid back-and-forth movements, and less than ten seconds later it tumbled to the ground, split neatly in half.

"They went through that timber as if it were butter," Joe said incredulously. "Smith must have worked as a lumberjack at one time."

Frank studied the camp director and Lafoote with renewed interest. "Teamwork like that takes plenty of practice," he declared. "Those two have obviously known each other for a while!"

Once their time was recorded, the men stepped aside for the next pair of contestants, and the Hardys ducked farther into the crowd of onlookers.

Soon the log-rolling event was announced. Chet and Biff had hoped to avoid the contest at the last minute, but Pierre had left them no choice. He had stationed the boys with two of his colleagues, who had kept a close eye on them while he was working with Larry Smith. Now, when their names were called, Lafoote all but pushed them out to the pond.

"Ladies and gents," the loudspeaker sounded, "we introduce two young men from down south—Mr. Chet Morton, and Mr. Biff Hooper!"

The crowd cheered as the boys reluctantly approached the pond. After paddling out to a large, floating log, they were supposed to climb on top of it and try to roll it with their feet until one of them fell into the water. The lumberjacks had shown their agility and skill and danced nimbly on the spinning log—sometimes for over

a minute—before one of them had slipped. But Chet and Biff were another story. They hardly managed to stand up on it before they both lost their balance and splashed wildly into the water.

"Well, that's the briefest log rolling *I've* ever seen," the announcer chortled. "Maybe they're just a little shy. Whaddaya say we give these guys another chance? After all, we've got to have a winner. That last match was a tie!"

"Yeah!" the crowd chorused, roaring with laughter. "Make 'em do it again."

Dripping wet and red-faced with embarrassment, the Bayport contestants slowly swam up to the log again.

"I don't think I can stand to watch." Joe winced. "They'll never forgive us for making them do this."

Chet and Biff climbed on the floating tree trunk and tried their best not to make fools out of themselves a second time. Luckily, Chet managed to keep his footing for a few seconds before falling in the water, and Biff—whose boxing training had taught him good balance—stayed on his end of the log long enough even to spin it several times before plummeting into the water.

"We have a winner!" the loudspeaker crackled. "Mr. Biff Hooper!"

The crowd cheered louder than it had for any

other event, but the two shaken contestants took no bows. Soaking wet, they scurried into the locker room as fast as they could. Neither of them came out until the ax-throwing contest was well under way. Even then, they were still too embarrassed to show their faces, and huddled next to the barracks behind a pile of logs.

"They're going to kill us when we get home," Frank said, grinning. "We'll have to make up for—"

Suddenly, a gasp of horror broke from the crowd. An ax head had flown off its handle and was hurtling through the air.

It hit the side of the red building, burying its razor-sharp edge just above the spot where Chet and Biff were sitting!

The Hardys jumped to their feet, staring at Pierre Lafoote, who held the ax handle in his right hand.

"Why, that . . . !" Joe growled, stepping forward with his fists clenched. "That was no accident."

Frank pulled his brother back, relieved that their friends were all right. "He may have let that ax fly on purpose, but he made a big mistake by doing it. Now we *know* he's Smith's accomplice!"

Joe sat down again. "So what'll we do?"

"Nothing yet," the dark-haired boy said quietly. "This contest isn't over until late this afternoon, and I don't think they'll try anything till then. Chet and Biff can stay and keep an eye on our suspects, but we should make Lafoote think his scare tactic worked, and leave."

"Where do you plan on going?" Joe asked. "Back to the camp?"

Frank grinned. "Don't you remember the errand Dad asked us to do for him at the biological research center? It's not far from here."

"Oh, brother, I forgot." Joe blushed. "We'd better get going."

The Hardys walked as casually as possible to the entrance of the red building, where they met Biff and Chet. After nearly being clobbered by the ax head, the two novice log rollers had all but forgotten their shame.

"This isn't your day, is it?" Joe teased. "We're sure glad you guys are all right. Did Lafoote say anything?"

"No. He just pulled the ax head out of the wood and grunted," Chet replied, shaken from the episode. "I wonder if he did it on purpose."

"He probably did," Frank said, then gave Biff a light punch on his shoulder. "You did us proud, you old log roller, you. You stayed on that thing longer than I could've, even if I'd been wearing cleats!"

The four boys had a good laugh in spite of the serious turn of events. "Listen," Joe broke in, "we have an errand to run for our father. Would you guys wait in the parking lot, and if either Lafoote or Smith leaves before we get back, try to follow him? But be careful. These guys are treacherous."

"Don't worry." Chet gulped. "We'll be *real* careful."

The Hardys drove to the highway and headed west. On the way, they discussed the case. "I bet Lafoote only entered the contest as a cover," Frank said. "His real mission was to kidnap George for the camp director, who set the whole thing up. Using the log jammer as a weapon, Lafoote probably went to the overnight campsite and confronted George, who didn't dare cry for help. Then, after stashing George safely away, Lafoote planted the T-shirt in the barn so the police would pin the abduction on the doomers."

"It all makes sense, except for one thing," Joe pondered. "If Smith wanted George for the money angle, why haven't the Watleys received a ransom note?"

"I don't know." Frank shrugged. "Maybe Smith and Lafoote are waiting to get George far away before they contact the parents. Or maybe Pierre's planning to take the boy with him after the contest."

The brothers were quiet for a while, each one following his own thoughts. Suddenly Joe called out, "Frank! There it is!" He pointed to a cluster of white buildings off the highway with a large sign in front of them that read VERMONT BIOLOGICAL RESEARCH CENTER.

Frank turned the car down an exit ramp. "Let's hope we can get the information Dad needs," he said.

6 Money Clue

The boys parked outside the main building and went into the lobby. The girl at the reception desk greeted them with a dimpled smile.

Frank introduced himself and his brother. "We're looking for Mr. Jeffrey Peters," he added.

The girl pushed a strawberry-blond curl away from her forehead. Her face was tanned and sprinkled with freckles.

"Oh, yes," she said. "Mr. Peters is in Building C on the sixth floor. Is he expecting you?"

"Yes."

The pretty receptionist swiveled in her desk chair and talked to the scientist on the intercom.

"Mr. Peters will see you in his lab," she said when she had finished. "Building C is next door. You can take the elevator to the sixth floor."

A few minutes later, the sleuths found themselves in a spacious white room equipped with modern biological research instruments. Jeffrey Peters was just winding up an experiment with a giant electron microscope. He was in his mid-fifties, with graying temples, and he was dressed in a white lab smock.

"Frank? Joe? Good to see you," he said, vigorously shaking their hands. "Sit down. What can I do for you?"

The Hardys took seats on lab stools and got right to the point.

"As you know, our father is looking for the last member of your genetic research team at NIH," Frank began. "Dad has located all the others, but Randolph Rhee seems to have disappeared. We understand you were a close associate of his."

"Yes." The scientist shrugged. "And ever since your father called, I've been racking my brain over this. You see, I ran into Randolph about a month ago on a train out of Boston. He told me he was retired, but he didn't tell me where he lived."

Frank leaned forward in his seat. "Did he say anything at all about what he was up to or where he was going?"

"No, I remember we only talked about the old days at NIH. It seems to me that Randolph didn't want to discuss the present very much."

"Try to recall your conversation with him if you can," Frank urged.

"Well, we discussed genetic engineering, mostly. He seemed very interested in that, especially the latest breakthroughs in the field. In fact, I was surprised how up-to-date he was on all the research, considering he'd retired some years before. I invited him here to the research center to give a lecture and meet some of my colleagues, but he refused. That's about it."

"You said you met him on a train," Joe took over. "Do you know where he was going? Did he have any luggage with him?"

"I got off before he did. I had been attending several lectures at Harvard University in Boston, after which I took the train back to Vermont. Randolph was still aboard when I got out. As far as luggage is concerned, I don't recall what he had with him. Several bags were on racks over our heads and I wouldn't have known which were his."

"When was the last time you spoke to Mr. Rhee before the train trip?" Frank asked.

Peters folded his hands behind his head and gazed out the window with a distant expression. "I hadn't seen him since the NIH project was discontinued ten years ago," he said wistfully. "Randolph was very upset about it. He was one of the head scientists, and he felt that we were on the brink of an amazing discovery in gene splicing. When the government decided the project was too dangerous and should be abandoned, Randolph was very bitter. He left without a word, and I haven't heard from him since, except that one time last month."

"What was it he felt you were on the verge of discovering?" Joe queried.

"Genetic engineering is one of the most exciting fields in modern biology," Peters said with a note of pride in his voice. "Inside every cell in our bodies are chromosomes which contain thousands of tiny genes. These genes are stacked together in a kind of code, which determines everything about us from our hair to our feet—our eye color, the shape of our nose, our physical build.

"What genetic engineers have been able to do

is to *alter* this code, so that someday we'll be able to create whole new life forms by arranging the genes in any way we want. Instead of waiting for nature and heredity to come up with two bright, ambitious boys such as yourselves, we'll actually be able to design you right in our laboratories!"

"That's frightening!" Joe exclaimed. "It sounds like you're playing God!"

"In a way, we are. That's why it's so exciting, and also why we have to be so careful about it."

"Is that what Randolph Rhee was after?" Frank asked, getting back to the point. "Creating new life forms?"

"He thought he was on the track." Peters nodded. "But don't worry, genetic research is still a long way from actually building humans from scratch. In our project, all we aimed to do was splice the very simple gene structure of bacteria, which is thousands of times easier to do than work on human chromosomes."

"And that's why the project was abandoned," Frank stated. "Because you created a potentially dangerous bacteria, which may still be alive in your bodies?"

"So the people at NIH say." The scientist

sighed. "But I really don't understand their reasoning. We all checked ourselves out for the bacteria then, and didn't find a trace. After your father called, I was examined again and the results were negative."

"Well, we still have to locate Mr. Rhee," Frank said. "As long as the government believes there's danger, we have to get to him as soon as possible."

"Agreed." Peters smiled. "And I'll contact you the minute I hear anything."

The Hardys stood up to go, and the white-smocked biologist escorted them to the door.

They left the lab and walked to the elevator, where they pressed the "Down" button and waited. Soon, the elevator doors opened and they stepped inside.

"Frank! Joe! Wait up!" they heard a voice call out just then.

Joe held the door open as running footsteps echoed down the hall, and Jeffrey Peters appeared. His eyes shone with excitement.

"I just remembered something else," he panted. "I knew there was a curious detail about my encounter with Rhee, but I just hadn't been able to bring it to mind."

The boys stepped back into the hall, waiting

eagerly for the man to catch his breath and explain.

"There was a snack cart on that train," the scientist said at last. "When the vendor came into our car, Randolph wanted a sandwich and a soda. When he paid for them, he gave the man Canadian money!"

"Are you sure it was Canadian currency?" Joe asked, excitedly.

"Yes! The man gave it back, telling Randolph he couldn't accept Canadian dollars. So Randolph had to search through his pockets to find some U.S. money."

"That may mean he lives in Canada." Frank beamed. "I'm sure glad you remembered!"

In high spirits, the Hardys said good-bye again and left the building.

"We ought to call Dad immediately and tell him about Randolph Rhee and his Canadian money," Joe said as they drove away from the biological research center.

The older Hardy boy checked his watch. "We'd better get back to the lumber camp. I bet the contest'll be over soon, and I don't want to risk losing our suspects."

Traveling as fast as the speed limit would allow, Frank and Joe cruised back to Green Mountain Park. When they arrived, an event was just winding up. Biff was still in the parking lot, hiding behind a green van.

"Where's Chet?" Frank asked as they pulled up next to their friend.

"He's following Smith in my Jeep!" Biff replied. "Smith left about twenty minutes ago with all the campers."

"What about Lafoote?" Joe inquired.

"He's still here. I've been watching."

"Quick! Duck down!" Frank said suddenly. "Here he comes now!"

7 *Stealthy Pursuit*

The French-Canadian had his ax slung over his shoulder and was looking furtively around as he crossed the parking lot. Frank and Joe slid down in their seats.

"Get in," Frank urged Biff, who had squatted next to the yellow sports sedan.

Luckily, there were so many cars in the lot that Lafoote didn't notice the boys. He turned toward the far end, striding up to a pale-blue two-door compact. When he climbed inside, Biff slid into the backseat of the Hardys'. yellow sedan.

"Be careful," Frank said to Joe, who was at the

65

wheel. "Lafoote will have his beady eyes open for anyone trailing him."

Joe waited until the blue compact was out of the park and on the road before throwing the sedan into gear. Then he stayed as far behind Lafoote as he could without losing him. They continued on the main highway for a long time, finally exiting on an interstate freeway toward Burlington, one of Vermont's largest cities.

"I hope he doesn't go too much farther," Joe remarked, nervously glancing at the gas gauge. "We only have an eighth of a tank left, which will take us another thirty miles at best."

The boys knew if they had to stop for gas, they'd lose the burly lumberjack and perhaps their only hope of finding George. By the time they reached Burlington, the gauge read close to empty.

Just then, the blue car turned up an exit ramp marked BUSINESS DISTRICT. Soon they were on a busy downtown avenue, and Joe had to use all his driving skills to trail Lafoote through traffic. Finally the compact pulled up in front of a train station.

"Phew!" Joe sighed, parking opposite the terminal. "That was too close for comfort!"

The needle was on "Empty." Another mile or

so and they would have run out of fuel for sure.

Frank peered out the window. "Okay. We've gotten this far. Let's not lose him now."

Lafoote had gone to the window of a rental car booth. Apparently, he was dropping off the blue compact before boarding a train.

Cautiously, the boys waited for Lafoote to finish up at the booth and disappear into the terminal before they got out of their own car and followed him.

"There." Joe pointed as they entered the station. "He's buying a ticket."

The boys ducked behind a bench in the waiting room until the lumberjack walked to the platform. They they rushed to the window and asked the clerk about Lafoote's destination.

"Can't tell you that," the man said stiffly. "It's against company policy. But I *can* tell you that the only train out of here in the next couple of hours leaves at five forty-three," he added with a wink.

"That's in twelve minutes," Joe said, checking his watch.

"And you and I'll be on it," Frank added. "Good thing I always carry a credit card. I'm not sure how much cash I have."

Not surprisingly, the train was going to

Canada, Lafoote's home territory. Frank and Joe bought two tickets to Montréal, which was the train's major stop. If Lafoote continued farther north, they would be able to purchase new tickets from the conductor.

"I don't understand," Biff said as he followed the sleuths toward a row of telephone booths. "What about George? Lafoote obviously doesn't have him."

"I know. But he may lead us to him," Frank replied as he reached for a phone. "I'm going to call Chet and Dad, then I want you to drive our car back to the lake. And don't forget to feed the old gas tank before you go."

Biff grinned. "Aye-aye, captain!"

Frank dailed the Hoopers' number. Chet was at the cottage, anxiously waiting to hear from the brothers.

"I followed Smith to Camp Ketchumken," he told Frank. "After he dropped off the kids, he left in a real hurry."

"Did you go after him?"

"No. Lieutenant Henderson took over at that point, trailing Smith in an unmarked police car. I haven't heard anything since."

"Okay. Now listen. Joe and I have to catch a train," Frank explained. "Biff will explain when he gets back to the cottage. See you later."

Frank clicked the receiver, slid another coin into the slot, and dialed the number of the police station. Lt. Henderson was there.

"I lost Smith," the detective admitted. "He must've been taking precautions because he pulled some pretty swift moves on the back roads. So I'm sure he had something to hide. I'm thinking of bringing him into the station for questioning."

"Could you hold off on that for a while?" Frank asked, explaining their plan to follow the French-Canadian lumberjack by train. "Lafoote doesn't have George, but I'm certain he and Smith are in cahoots on this kidnapping. I think if we stay close to him we'll find out something. And I'd rather not scare him off by arresting Smith."

"I'm not sure I understand what you're hoping to learn," Henderson said. "But you've been right on the mark so far. I'll let you handle this your way. Just remember to stay in close contact with me."

"We will," Frank promised. "One more thing. You said you'd rounded up several members of that Apocalypse cult. Do you still have them at the station?"

"Yes."

"Think I could speak to one of them?"

"Of course," the detective replied. "Hold on."

Frank heard Henderson put down the receiver. He glanced at Joe, who held up five fingers, indicating that only five minutes were left before the train was due to depart.

"Hello?" a female voice spoke up after thirty seconds had gone by. She sounded like a woman in her twenties or early thirties.

"You belong to the Apocalypse cult?" Frank queried.

"Yes," she answered hesitantly.

"Well, I'm Frank Hardy, one of the people you tried to hire to track down the missing camper," he explained. "Your leader told us about Satan in the north country, building an army of giants. He also mentioned a river that runs both ways. Can you give us a better description than that? It would be a big help in finding George and getting the pressure off you and your friends."

The woman was quiet for a moment, as if considering whether she should trust Frank. Then she said, "I know nothing more than what our leader has already told you. The Devil is far up a river that flows in two directions, where few men dare to go, and where he builds his army."

"That's it?"

"He lives deep in a forest, a dark forest. Is that any help?"

"It might be," Frank replied. "Thanks."

Once again, he hung up and fished another coin out of his pocket. By now, Joe was holding up three fingers!

"Hello, Dad?" Frank said after placing a collect call to Bayport. "We came up with something at the biological research center. Peters says he saw Randolph Rhee on a train from Boston about a month ago. Rhee never told him where he lived—only that he was retired—but Peters finally recalled that Rhee was carrying Canadian currency."

"Good work, son," Mr. Hardy replied. "This may be the break I needed. Now it's even more important that I locate Rhee."

"Why, Dad? It's been ten years since that genetic engineering project broke up, and Peters said he can't see how anyone could still carry the bacteria."

"Because there's more to this case than I originally told you," Mr. Hardy said gravely. "That story about the deadly bacteria was just a pretense to round up the scientists. The real story is much more bizarre. But it's also top secret, and I can't fill you in until I get special government clearance to do so. Call me in the morning and I'll—"

"That's okay, Dad," Frank interrupted his father. "I've got to run. The Montreal train is leaving now and our kidnapping suspect is on it!"

Outside the phone booth, Joe was waving and frantically pointing at his wristwatch. The train was about to pull out.

Frank hung up, bid a hasty farewell to Biff, and bolted through the terminal with Joe in the lead. Seconds later, the Hardys jumped onto the train, just as it started to roll.

"What if Lafoote sees us?" Joe panted as the train gained speed.

"We'll have to hide," Frank decided. "Come on!"

Frank and Joe slipped into the train's tiny washroom and quickly locked the door.

"I wish we'd had time to rig up disguises," Joe said.

"Lafoote may have seen us already," Frank mused. "But I doubt it. This train is at least eight or nine cars long, and we got into the last one."

The brothers waited until they were out of the city and rolling through open country. Then Frank unlocked the washroom door and cracked it open an inch.

"All clear," he whispered.

The boys left their stuffy hiding place and

took seats in the rear of the car, where they had a good view out the window and could see anyone getting on or off the train. A few loggers who had participated in the contest sat nearby, but none seemed to recognize the boys.

"Now, as long as Lafoote doesn't decide to take a stroll back here, we'll be okay," Frank remarked, as he eased back in his seat and watched the rugged mountains roll by.

The long train chugged northward. Soon the orange sun set in the sky, and most of the passengers began to doze off. Others went forward to the snack bar for food. The Hardys, though, stayed glued to their seats. It wasn't likely that the bearded French-Canadian would be getting off before Montreal, but they didn't want to take any chances. At every station they watched passengers disembark, and were ready to hurry off the train themselves if necessary.

It was well past midnight when the conductor appeared and announced, "Next stop, Montreal. Passengers going farther north, please move up to the first three cars!"

"Uh-oh," Joe groaned. "They're shortening the train."

"Let's just hope Lafoote gets off here," Frank said, "or else we'll be sitting ducks."

"You mean Canada geese?" Joe cracked.

The train slowly came to a stop at the station and, one by one, the passengers filed out, either to leave the train or to move forward. Frank and Joe stayed in their seats and looked out the window.

"Didn't you boys hear my announcement?" the conductor called out, checking to make sure no one remained in the back section. "If you're going on, you'll have to move up front. All cars except the first three are being disconnected."

The Hardys hesitated before getting up, quickly rechecking their window. Many people were on their way to the terminal, but the burly lumberjack wasn't among them.

"I guess we stay on the train," Frank finally decided, and he and Joe hurried toward the third car. Again, they hid in the washroom.

"What'll we do now?" Joe asked nervously. "We can't stay in this stuffy room forever, and Lafoote is bound to see us if we try to find seats."

Frank went outside and peered around the corner, studying the passengers. Nearly all were lumberjacks, and among them was Pierre Lafoote! He was sitting in an aisle seat near the other end of the car, with his back to Frank.

The young detective was about to return to the washroom when there was a jolt that almost knocked him down. Through the window in the rear door, he saw that a freight car had been attached to the train. A moment later, the train pulled out of the station with a screech.

Frank returned to his brother and told him what he had seen.

"What'll we do?" Joe asked. "Grab him now?"

Frank shook his head. "No. He wouldn't admit anything; we can't prove anything; and it would only warn him that we're on to him."

Joe nodded. "So what's the next step?"

"We'll have to get out of this car, that's for sure," Frank said. "I have a plan. Follow me."

The boys slipped out of the washroom and Frank furtively opened the door at the rear end of their car. He stepped onto the narrow steel walkway. "I think we'll be safe here," he said, as he sat down on the ledge.

Joe huddled next to his brother and they watched as the bright lights of Montreal began to disappear in the distance. A host of stars lit up the night sky, and a cold wind made the boys shiver. Soon they could only see the dark outline of a forest on either side of the tracks.

After a while, Frank stood up and looked through the window in the back door of the passenger car.

"Guess what? Everyone's asleep in there."

"That's not surprising." Joe yawned. "I wish I were inside with them, nice and comfortable!"

"Don't you see?" Frank went on. "This might be our lucky break. With all those guys dozing, we can sneak back in without being noticed."

Joe nodded. "It's risky, but it beats freezing to death out here," he said.

The boys crept noiselessly back into the train. The exhausted lumberjacks were sprawled in their seats, all with their eyes closed. The Hardys made their way stealthily down the aisle, careful to keep their balance.

When they got to Lafoote, he was snoring with his mouth wide open. Frank stooped down next to him and, as gently and deftly as he could, reached into the man's jacket pocket. He pulled out its contents: a wallet, a passport, and a claim check.

Splitting the material between them, the boys quickly memorized as much of it as they could, then Frank replaced the items, and they tiptoed back down the aisle and settled themselves in the last seat. They pulled out their notepads and jotted down their information.

"I got his passport and wallet," Frank whispered. "His full name is Pierre Burnaise Lafoote, and he lives in Saskatoon, Saskatchewan. There was no street address. In his wallet he had some money and his train ticket, which was marked Sligo Tressel. The ticket was handwritten, so Sligo Tressel must be a flag stop. What did you find?"

The blond boy grinned. "That pink claim check was for a railroad freight delivery. The destination on it was also Sligo Tressel! I got the claim number."

Frank stared at the number scrawled on Joe's pad—947628.

"But Lafoote didn't have anything with him other than his suitcase when we saw him at the Burlington station! If he was shipping something big enough for freight, he would've—"

"Exactly," Joe broke in. "He either dropped it off earlier or someone else did it for him. Like Smith, for instance."

Frank jumped to his feet. "We have to get into that freight car!" he cried in a hushed voice.

"Well, we can't do it while the train is moving," Joe warned.

"You're right," Frank said and sat down again. The brothers waited anxiously for the next stop, hoping it wouldn't be Sligo Tressel.

Finally, they pulled up to a small wilderness depot, and to the Hardys' relief, the sign in front of it read TIMBERVILLE. The instant the train came to a halt, they jumped out the door and scurried to the freight car. Joe unlatched the door and they climbed inside.

"I hope nobody saw us," he panted as he closed the heavy door, leaving them in total darkness. Frank stumbled over crates and boxes until he found a light switch. By the time the train started up again, the boys were already searching the freight for a number that matched Lafoote's claim check.

"I found it!" Joe finally cried from a corner of the car. "Come on. Let's get it open before it's too late!"

He pointed at a very large rectangular wooden crate. Holes had been drilled in its side, and the lid was nailed shut. Frantically, the boys looked for something to use to pry it open.

"Rats!" Frank murmured, seeing nothing. "Where's a crowbar when you need one?"

"We'll have to break this thing open with our bare hands!" Joe decided. "There are only six nails. I bet we can do it."

Each boy grabbed a corner of the lid and tugged with all his might.

After several attempts, the cover pulled free and the Hardys gasped.

Inside the crate was the crumpled body of a young boy!

9 A Tale of Supermen

"It must be George!" Joe cried out.

Frank grabbed the boy's limp left arm and felt for a pulse. "He's alive!" he exclaimed. "Probably he's been sedated! Help me get him out of this thing."

With a groan, the Hardys lifted the heavy, unconscious youth from the wooden crate and set him on the floor of the boxcar.

"George! George! Wake up!" Joe said, and gently slapped the boy's face to revive him.

George was dressed in a light-gray sweat suit, presumably the one he'd been wearing at the campsite. On his feet were a pair of blue sneakers. His hair was reddish brown, and he had the same button nose and high cheekbones as his mother. But he was built like his father, tall and broad, with powerful shoulders and legs.

"It's not working," Frank said, when George did not respond to Joe's slaps. "Come on, we'd better take him outside before the train leaves." He replaced the lid of the crate, then returned to the boy.

Cradling the young camper in their arms, Frank and Joe dragged him to the door of the boxcar and carefully lowered him to the tracks. They didn't dare go out on the platform side, afraid that they might be seen by Lafoote. A moment later, the train started up again. With a loud hiss of steam, it slowly disappeared from sight.

"What are we going to do about Lafoote?" Joe said. "I hate to just let him get away."

"We'll have to forget about him for now. George is far more important."

The brothers dragged the unconscious boy away from the tracks, laying him on a damp patch of grass. The gray, early-morning sky was growing brighter by the minute, and a light dew covered the ground. Only the chirping of a few early birds broke the silence.

Joe looked around. Aside from the shacklike train depot, the Canadian countryside seemed to

stretch on forever without even a hint of civiliza-
tion. "Where do you think we are?"

Frank knelt down and began swabbing
George's face with a dew-drenched bandana. "I
don't know. We'll have to get a map of this area."

Suddenly, the camper twitched and he let out
a low groan. A second later, his eyes flickered
open and he stared at the dark-haired sleuth
with a glazed look of fear.

"How are you feeling, George?" Frank asked.

Without answering, the boy struggled to get
up and run away. But he was still too weak, and
fell back on the grass.

"What . . . who . . . where? . . ." he muttered.

"Take it easy," Frank said reassuringly.
"You're safe now. We just rescued you from that
horrible lumberjack. You'll be going home
soon."

The twelve-year-old gazed from one Hardy to
the other and grinned weakly. "Home?" he
asked.

"Yes, home," Joe said.

In a few minutes, George was up and walking
around. The sun was breaking over the treetops
as the trio crossed the tracks and made their way
to the depot.

Frank opened the door and stepped inside.

"Didn't anybody ever teach you any manners?" a man snapped gruffly. "You're supposed to knock before going in someone's house!"

Taken by surprise, the Hardys stopped and looked around the shack's interior. A potbellied stove was in one corner, and the walls were hung with deer antlers. In another corner were several chairs and a cot, which was occupied by an old man with curly white whiskers and a protruding paunch. He was in his undershorts, and was modestly holding a sleeping bag up to cover himself.

"Sorry." Frank reddened. "I didn't know—"

"You didn't know anybody lived here!" the cranky old man interrupted. "So you just barged in like you owned the place. Well, now that you're in, you might as well sit down and make yourselves at home."

While he hurriedly stepped into a pair of pants and put on a shirt, the boys sat in the chairs. They learned that the man's name was Luke and that he was the depot attendant. They also found out that the next train going south wouldn't come for another two hours.

"Now, if you're done askin' questions," Luke said, "may I ask what you kids are doin' here?"

"That's a long story," Frank answered. "George here got on the wrong train and we . . . ah . . . had to get him back."

The old-timer stared at the tall boy. "You sure are a big kid, ain't you?" He guffawed. "You aren't one of Paul Bunyan's grandchildren by any chance?"

"Wh-who?" the young camper stammered, still a little dizzy.

"Paul Bunyan!" Luke repeated. "Don't you know he was the greatest lumberjack who ever lived? Him and his blue ox, Babe, used to cut and haul more timber in one day than a hundred regular men could handle in a whole month! He was taller than the tallest sequoia tree. The only problem was, it took a whole grain mill workin' day and night just to make enough flour for his breakfast. Paul, he just loved his flapjacks, though, and he couldn't get enough of 'em in the mornin' before cuttin' timber."

Frank and Joe could barely suppress smiles as they listened to the story. They'd both heard the legend of Paul Bunyan, a mighty-muscled bearded giant, who was famed to have felled whole forests in one morning.

"Come on." Joe laughed. "You don't believe there really was such a man, do you?"

"Believe?" Luke howled, jumping off the cot. "I saw him with my own two eyes many a time. In fact, *I* was the one who had to look after the blue ox's stable. Old Babe measured forty-two ax handles and a plug of chewin' tobacco between the horns! You just try bringin' in two tons of oats every day just to feed him, then tell me you don't believe!"

"Okay, okay." Frank rolled his eyes. "We believe you. But George is not Bunyan's grandson."

The depot attendant shrugged. "Well, maybe he ain't, but with all the stories goin' 'round these days, I thought I'd ask."

The brothers both leaned forward in their chairs.

"Stories?" Joe queried. "What kind of stories?"

"I've heard that some of Bunyan's kinfolk are still livin' to the north," the old man replied. "I haven't actually seen any of them, but I hear they're hidin' out in the forest and don't want nobody to go botherin' 'em. It's supposed to be a big secret, so you won't hear folks talkin' about it much."

"Do you have any idea just where this Bunyan clan is located?" Joe pressed, his curiosity growing.

The old man shook his head. "No, I don't."

"Do you know where Sligo Tressel is?" Frank took over.

"Oh, 'bout thirty miles farther up the tracks,"

Luke replied with a puzzled look. "Why?"

"Oh . . . uhmmm . . . we heard it was a good place to go camping," Frank fumbled.

"Is there a telephone around here?" Joe asked.

"Telephone?" Luke asked, smiling and exposing the few teeth he had left. "I haven't seen one of those things for six or seven years."

"We'll take George back to Montreal," Frank told his brother. "We can contact Dad and Henderson from there."

The Hardys were as eager as George to let everyone know he was safe and on his way home. His parents had been through enough without prolonging their worries and heartbreak any more than necessary.

Thanking Luke for his hospitality, the boys left the shack and sat on the grass near the tracks to wait for the train. They went over everything that had happened, comparing notes.

As the Hardys had guessed, Lafoote had kidnapped George from the campsite.

With the steel-pointed log jammer, he had forced the boy from his sleeping bag that fateful night. The groove in the dirt had been made when Lafoote had demonstrated what he'd do to George if he tried to cry for help or escape.

"Boy, I was scared when he marched me through the woods!" The young camper shuddered.

Joe nodded. "You must've been. Where did he take you, George?"

"A hideout in the forest. When we got there, he tied me up and left."

"Probably he doubled back to the old barn where the Apocalypse people were holding their meeting," Frank deduced. "When it was over, he snuck inside and planted your T-shirt that he had taken from the campsite to make it appear that the cult had abducted you. It was a clever frame-up."

George had been tied up in the hideout for a day. Then Lafoote had come and injected him with a sedative.

"I can't remember anything after that," George said sadly.

"Well, he must have put you in the crate, and taken you to the Burlington train station just before the lumberjack competition, for shipment to Sligo Tressel on the evening train," Frank said. "After the contest was over, he boarded the train himself, planning to unload the crate when he reached his destination."

Joe grinned. "I wish I could see Lafoote's face

when he unloads that crate. He's in for a Bunyan-sized surprise!"

"Let's hope he thinks George escaped all by himself," Frank cautioned. "Otherwise he'll know we're hot on his trail."

"Here comes the train!" George exclaimed, pointing down the tracks at a pair of headlights glowing bright and yellow in the gray morning mist.

A sudden thought stuck Joe. "I hope Lafoote isn't on it. He could've decided to take the first train back when he found the crate empty."

"We'll have to take that chance," Frank said, wearily getting to his feet.

10   Mr. Hardy Needs Help

The train rolled to a stop at the depot and the three boys got on. When they had made sure the French-Canadian wasn't aboard, Frank and Joe curled up in seats and fell fast asleep. They didn't wake up again until George shook them at noontime.

"Hey, you guys," the camper said. "We're almost in Montreal."

Frank's eyes opened and he smiled lazily at George. Only hours earlier he'd eagerly shaken the boy from a deep slumber himself!

"Here's what we'll do," he said. "We'll put you on a train to Burlington, then we'll call

Lieutenant Henderson, who will arrange for your parents to pick you up."

"You won't come with me?" George asked anxiously.

"No, George, we can't. We'll have to go after Lafoote. But don't worry, we'll make sure you're safe," Frank told the young boy.

After George was on his way to Vermont and the detective had been notified of the latest events, Frank and Joe went to a travel bureau in the train station and bought a map of Canada. Spreading it out on a table, they perused the wilderness area north of Montreal. Sligo Tressel was not marked on the map, but the brothers identified other stops the train had made on its route through the province of New Brunswick.

"Lafoote could be anywhere in here," Frank remarked, drawing a wide circle with his finger around the upper half of New Brunswick.

Joe whistled. "That's a lot of territory to cover. Maybe we ought to rent an airplane and survey it from above."

"There'd be no place to land," Frank observed, staring at the green blotch on the map that indicated unbroken forest. "Our best bet is to take a train to Sligo Tressel, and play it by ear from there."

He stood up and the boys returned to the phone booth to call their home in Bayport. "Hello?" a woman answered.

"Hi, Aunt Gertrude," Frank said, recognizing the voice of their favorite relative. "How are you? Where's Dad?"

Gertrude Hardy had taken up permanent residence in her brother's household some time ago. Though she hid her real feelings behind a stern disposition, she was very fond of her nephews and proud of their reputation as amateur detectives.

"Where are *you*?" she snapped. "You're supposed to be on a nice, quiet vacation in Vermont, and the next thing I hear, you're both off in Canada chasing after kidnappers!"

"Don't worry about us," Frank assured the flustered woman. "We're not in any trouble. But we told Dad we'd call him this morning."

"I know that! And now it's past noon. I was sure you boys were lying in a ditch somewhere! You've had us all plenty worried, I tell you."

"Sorry," Frank apologized. "We just couldn't get to a phone before now, honest. Where's Dad?"

"Your father had to catch a plane. But he left a message for you. He wants you to go to Halifax,

Nova Scotia, where you're supposed to meet a Mr. Chester at Flannigan's Hotel. He says for you to drop whatever you're doing to make it there. It's very important."

"Did he say who this Mr. Chester is or why we're to see him?" Frank asked.

"No, but if your father says it's important, it's important," Aunt Gertrude said seriously.

"Okay. If Dad calls, tell him we're on our way. And try not to worry too much about us."

Frank rang off and related his conversation to Joe.

"I guess we'll have to give up chasing Lafoote for a while," he said. "That means we'll probably lose him for good. I hope Dad's mission is as important as he says."

Again, the brothers opened their map and found Nova Scotia. Except for its northern tip, it was separated from the Canadian mainland by the Bay of Fundy, making it almost a huge island by itself.

"We'll have to fly there," Joe stated. "Otherwise it'll take too long." The boys took a taxi to the airport just outside the city limits. They were able to catch a flight to Halifax, Nova Scotia's major city and seaport, within an hour. By late afternoon, they were circling the Halifax harbor as the plane eased in for a landing.

From the air, the city appeared to be a striking blend of old and new. There were churches and stone fortifications dating back two centuries; there were modern skyscrapers and sleek, new navy warships in the harbor.

"Well, whatever else happens, I'd enjoy doing some sightseeing while we're here," Frank commented, gazing out the airplane's window.

Upon arrival, the boys caught a shuttle bus to the downtown area. They found Flannigan's Hotel near the docks and walked into the lobby.

A tall, handsome man in his mid-forties with graying temples called to them from a lounge chair.

"Dad!" Joe blurted. "What are you doing here? Your message said—"

Fenton Hardy waved off his son's question. "I thought you might get here before me," he explained. "So I wanted to make sure you and Mr. Chester would find each other."

A man who was seated beside the famous detective stood up. He was a short, slight man dressed in a neat, pin-striped suit. His gray-blue eyes gave a pleasant expression to his face.

"Frank, Joe." Mr. Chester smiled faintly as he shook their hands. "Glad to meet you. Now if we can all sit down, I'll tell you why we've asked you here."

The boys took seats next to the men and Mr. Chester went on in a hushed tone. "I work for the United States government. I'm with the Central Intelligence Agency."

"The CIA?" Joe's jaw dropped open. He knew that the CIA was a branch of the government concerned with international security operations, whose functions included guarding the United States against foreign espionage.

"Let me get to the point," Mr. Chester went on. "Your father told you about the scientists we've hired him to track down, but he hasn't informed you of our real reasons for wanting them. Thanks to you boys, we now believe that one of the men, Randolph Rhee, is connected with a foreign power that is planning to use genetic engineering for . . . let's say . . . unethical purposes."

"What country?" Joe broke in eagerly.

"I can't tell you that for security reasons," the CIA agent replied. "But I can tell you that this particular country has been known to use unfair and illegal methods in past Olympic games— such as drugging athletes to make them run faster, or injecting male hormones into women to give them stronger builds. Because of this, we've had undercover agents keeping a close eye on the country's Olympic program."

Mr. Chester paused for a moment, and when he spoke again, his voice was almost a whisper. "Recently we've discovered that the country is planning to use genetic engineering to produce superathletes. I know it's hard to believe, but all signs suggest that they are actually working on a design of superhumans which they will use at future Olympic games. It's our job to put a stop to this before it's too late."

"Wow!" Joe muttered. "Test-tube athletes."

"Exactly." The agent nodded. "If it's not controlled right from the start, genetic engineering of humans might well lead to the mass production of robot people for all kinds of purposes."

"But Dr. Peters at the Vermont Biological Research Center told us that genetic research was still a long way from that sort of thing," Frank remarked.

Chester shrugged. "That's why we can't figure out how this foreign power is doing it. Perhaps there are breakthroughs in the field that nobody knows about but them. That's why we checked into the old NIH scientists. The team included some of the most brilliant minds in genetic engineering. If any scientists were capable of making a major discovery in the field, they'd be the ones to do it."

"So you think the foreign country has hired Randolph Rhee to produce the superathletes?" Joe said, now on the edge of his chair.

"At first, we just had a hunch," the agent explained. "But when we managed to locate all the scientists except Mr. Rhee, our suspicions grew. Nobody seemed to know where he was or what he was doing. When you boys found out from Jeffrey Peters that he'd seen Rhee on a northbound train carrying Canadian currency, we were almost certain our hunch was right. You see, the foreign country has been sending a man on secret trips to Canada."

"I do see," Frank spoke up. "But I don't understand what you need us for."

Mr. Chester cleared his throat. "Our undercover agent in that foreign country learned last night that a man is flying into Halifax tonight. We want to follow him and see if he leads us to Rhee, but it wouldn't be safe. If I or any other agent was caught tailing the man, it could create a sticky international situation. It's a long story, but basically the Canadian government doesn't want to have to answer for an American agent operating on Canadian turf. It would create a diplomatic mess. But if you boys were to follow the man, you could be caught without embarrassment to anybody. You'd just be a couple of nosy youngsters, and no one would take you seriously."

"That's our specialty"—Frank grinned—"not being taken seriously."

Joe scratched his head. "Okay, where do we begin?"

Mr. Chester drew a photograph out of his jacket pocket and handed it to the sleuths. It showed an olive-skinned man with straight black hair and a thin mustache.

"His name is Candir Karu," the agent revealed. "He'll be landing at Halifax Airport sometime tonight. My phone number is on the back of the photo. I'll be staying here at the hotel with your father and can provide you with any assistance you need. I already have a four-wheel-drive Jeep ready for you."

Frank studied the photo, then slipped it into his shirt pocket.

"Karu will be trying to cover his tracks," Mr. Chester went on. "But I know you two are experts at trailing people, so I'm counting on you not to lose him. If he leads us to Mr. Rhee, we should be able to put an end to their scheme once and for all."

Frank stood up. "We'll get right out to the airport."

"Good." Mr. Chester smiled.

Fenton Hardy, who had kept quiet through the whole conversation, finally spoke up. "I packed a couple of bags for you in Bayport. And I think it would be a good idea for you to put on something else before you took off."

Caught up in the excitement, the boys had forgotten that they hadn't changed their clothes in two days. Their shirts and khakis were wrinkled and dirty.

"Thanks, Dad." Frank laughed. "One more day in these duds and Karu would know someone was on his trail by the scent alone!"

The young detectives went to their father's room to shower, and a half hour later were on their way to the airport in the Jeep.

Joe stopped outside the passenger terminal, where they had a clear view of anyone coming out of the building.

"I hope Mr. Karu checks into a hotel for the night," he said, biting into one of the tunafish sandwiches Mr. Hardy had gotten for them. "I'm still pretty pooped!"

Frank downed a bottle of orange soda. "Same here. I sure could use a little shut-eye."

Just then, an olive-skinned man emerged from the terminal. He had a thin mustache and was carrying a large briefcase!

"There he is!" Joe cried.

11   *The Elusive Scientist*

Candir Karu seemed to sense he was being watched. He glanced furtively around, his eyes settling for an instant on the Jeep. Then he hailed a taxi.

"This won't be easy!" Frank groaned as the cab pulled out of the airport terminal.

Joe smiled dryly. "Nothing worthwhile ever is." Stuffing the rest of the tunafish sandwich into his mouth, he swung out of their parking space and followed the foreigner's cab, keeping well behind.

The taxi led the Hardys straight into downtown Halifax, finally depositing its passenger at a place called Bagpipe Inn.

"So far, so good," Frank said as they parked in a movie theater lot next to the inn. "Maybe he'll stay here all night and we can get some rest."

Karu did spend the night in the Bagpipe Inn, and the brothers took turns sleeping in the Jeep. Early the next morning, though, the foreigner strode briskly out the door and went down the street.

"Wake up, Joe," Frank urged. "He's on the move again. We'll have to follow him on foot."

The city streets were filled with early rush-hour traffic, and the sidewalks were crowded with Nova Scotians on their way to work. The Hardys walked at a quick trot, dodging pedestrians to stay with Karu. Several blocks later, they saw him cut into a narrow alley and disappear from sight.

Frank broke into a run. "Come on, or we'll lose him."

They turned the corner and hurried into the alley. Except for trash cans lined up along a brick wall, it was empty!

"Where in the world—" Joe began, when he suddenly felt a hand grab the back of his shirt collar and jerk him to a stop. A second later, he felt the sharp blade of a knife against his spine!

"Who are you working for?" a thickly accented voice hissed over his shoulder.

The knife pushed harder into Joe's back, and the man pressed his arm against Joe's throat in a tight headlock.

"What do you mean?" the boy gagged. "I'm not working for anyone!"

Frank, who had been in the lead, wheeled around and saw his brother in Karu's grasp. Quickly he came to Joe's aid.

"Please, sir," he pleaded in his most innocent tone of voice. "We weren't going to rob you, honest. We just want our money back for those phony watches you sold us last week."

The foreigner appeared flustered. "What watches?" he snapped. "Why were you punks following me?"

"This isn't the guy," Joe choked, picking up his brother's cue. "The guy we got them from looked the same, but he had a French accent."

"Sorry, mister," Frank added, taking a step forward. "We thought you were the man who sold us a couple of gold watches last week. He told us they were genuine, but when we got home we found out they were just plated. We decided we'd try to get our money back, but—"

"That's enough!" Karu blurted angrily. "And if

you come one step closer, you'll see the end of this knife sticking out of your friend's belly!"

Without relaxing his grip, the foreign agent picked the boy's wallet out of Joe's back pocket and thumbed through it with one hand.

"What are you kids doing in Nova Scotia?" he queried, seeing from Joe's license that he was from the United States.

"We're on summer vacation from school," Frank replied truthfully. "We're visiting our grandmother," he added. "She lives here."

Karu hesitated a moment, then, with a look of disgust, he shoved Joe away from him. "Very well, then," he spat. "Go home to Grandma. But if you were lying to me, you're both dead. Understand?"

The boys nodded with frightened faces.

The mustached foreigner dropped Joe's wallet in the gutter and hurried out of the alley. Quickly he disappeared in the crowd.

"Good acting job," Joe complimented his brother. He stooped down to retrieve his billfold.

Frank grinned. "The question is, what'll we do now? If Karu spots us again, he won't be fooled, and that will leave him with only two options—to call off his meeting with Rhee, or kill us. Either way, we lose."

Joe shuddered at the memory of the steel point in his back. "But we can't just let that creep get away," he muttered.

The Hardy boys left the alley and gazed at the busy street. Karu was nowhere in sight, but at the end of the block was something that gave Frank an idea.

"Come on," he said excitedly. "I might have the perfect solution to our problem."

He walked toward an old stone fortification the boys had spied from the air. Years ago, it must have been built to guard the entrance to the harbor. Now much of it was in ruins, but the rest served as an attraction for tourists. What had caught Frank's eye was a high terrace on the fort that overlooked the harbor and the streets below. From it, rows of mortar cannons had once blasted enemy warships out of the harbor. Now it was a scenic lookout point with rows of pay telescopes lined up along its edge.

Frank and Joe raced down the street, then paid a dollar each to visit the stone fort. They sprinted up to the terrace, where they fed quarters into two telescopes and scanned the city below for the face of Candir Karu.

"Bingo!" Joe exclaimed, after a moment behind the lens. "I've got him!"

Following his brother's aim, Frank pointed

his telescope to a spot near the docks. Briefcase in hand, the foreign agent could be seen stepping into a fishing boat. Once he was aboard, the gangplank was raised and two crewmen began casting off its lines.

"Oh, no!" Joe cried. "No sooner have we found him than we lose him!"

"Don't you worry about a thing. Just keep that fishing boat in sight until you've used up every quarter we've got," Frank decided. "I'm going to call Mr. Chester and see if he can dig up a boat for us, too!"

Feeding money into the telescope, Joe watched the fishing vessel while Frank ran to the nearest pay phone and dialed the number the federal agent had given him.

"I was afraid something like this might happen," Mr. Chester said when he heard Frank's story. "Go to the end of pier six, off Lower Water Street. You'll find a lobster boat there owned by a man named Phillipe. Just tell him your names and he'll take you wherever you have to go."

"Thanks," Frank said. "We'll contact you the first chance we get."

He rang off, and raced back to the lookout terrace, where he related the news to Joe.

"Great!" his brother exclaimed, looking up from the telescope. "I've followed Karu's boat. It turned south down the coast."

Twenty minutes later, the Hardys were on their way out of the harbor in a spanking-new lobster boat. A stiff easterly breeze was bringing in big, rolling swells from the Atlantic, and when their boat turned south it caught the swells broadside and rocked violently. The captain, a jolly man, had no trouble handling the surf, though, and used his two powerful engines to cut through the waves at a good and steady clip.

Standing in the bow, both Frank and Joe strained their eyes toward the horizon.

"I think I see Karu," the older boy remarked, picking out the rigging of a fishing vessel several miles ahead.

Joe peered through a pair of binoculars. "That's him, all right. We shouldn't get too much closer than we are now."

Phillipe cut the engines down a third and they followed Karu at a safe distance.

"I wonder where he's headed," Joe commented, now drenched with the salty ocean spray that kicked up around the bow.

"Beats me," Frank replied. "I just hope he doesn't see us."

The fishing vessel continued to the tip of Nova Scotia, then turned west. By midafternoon, it had angled away from the coast altogether, setting a course across the Bay of Fundy. Finally, it reached the shores of New Brunswick and docked at a small fishing village.

"Throttle her up!" Frank called to the cabin. "I don't want to lose him ashore!"

Phillipe gunned his engines, and the lobster boat chugged into the dock five minutes later. Karu was nowhere in sight.

"Rats!" Joe grumbled. "He probably had a car waiting for him and is long gone."

"Maybe, and maybe not," Frank said thoughtfully. "Let's go ashore and ask a few questions."

The brothers walked into the tiny village. There was only one road through the place, and a group of old men were sitting along the edge of it, at work cleaning their day's haul of fish.

"Have you seen a stranger around here in the past ten minutes?" Frank inquired. "He may have been driving down this road."

"You mean a foreign-looking guy?" one of the men asked.

"Yes," Joe said eagerly. "Did you see him?"

"He walked by here all right," the man replied.

The brothers bolted away, waving their thanks to the fishermen. The road arched inland up a long hill, and by the time they reached its top, they were panting with exhaustion. Yet there was no sign of Karu anywhere. They could see the road ahead of them for almost a mile, but it was deserted!

"Where did he go?" Joe cried in frustration as he tried to catch his breath.

Frank looked puzzled. "I don't have a clue. Let's go back to the boat. We can call Mr. Chester on the radio and at least give him an idea where Karu was headed."

They returned to the village, feeling defeated. As they rounded a bend, they suddenly spotted a lone figure coming toward them. Joe was about to duck into a clump of bushes, but his brother stopped him.

"It's Phillipe!" Frank cried. "Come on!"

The captain was jogging up to them, waving his arms frantically.

"Hurry! Hurry! To the boat!" he yelled, then turned around and headed toward the harbor.

Summoning what strength they had left, the Hardys ran after him until they were back at the boat. As they climbed aboard, Phillipe threw off the lines and started the engines.

"What's going on?" Frank blurted.

"Look!" Phillipe exclaimed, pointing to the spot where Karu's fishing boat had been. "It's gone! And the foreigner went with it! I waited and waited for you so we could follow him, but you did not come for so long!"

The Hardys were stunned. The stopover in the tiny fishing village had just been a clever ploy to shake them. Karu had purposely walked down the road so they would try to follow him, then he'd doubled back through the woods to his boat and taken off!

"He spotted us," Frank groaned. "Now he'll go straight to Rhee and warn him."

Churning the waters up in a foamy froth, the lobster boat's propellers spun at full capacity as Phillipe maneuvered the craft from the dock.

"Do you think we can catch up with him?" Joe asked.

The captain frowned. "If we're lucky, maybe. We know the direction he took."

For the next hour, they followed the coast with no luck. There was no sign of the fishing vessel anywhere. The sun was beginning to sink, and the Hardys' hopes of ever finding Karu again were sinking with it.

"I'm going to take her into St. John," Phillipe said at last. "Sorry, boys, but soon it will be night and I'm dangerously low on fuel. St. John is the only good port in this area."

Joe climbed on top of the cabin for one last look around with the binoculars. The fading sunlight glimmered orange on the Bay of Fundy, and a few sails stood out on the horizon. But no fishing boats were visible. In the distance, the city of St. John loomed over the coastline.

In the cabin, Frank spread out a nautical chart and studied it. The New Brunswick coast was dotted with coves, and St. John's harbor was connected to several large estuaries and a long river leading inland. The fishing vessel could have taken refuge anywhere, and by night it would be impossible to find.

"Maybe Karu had to make a refueling stop in St. John himself," the boy said hopefully.

Phillipe shook his head. "They filled up at the village."

"What about this river?" Frank inquired, pointing to the long line leading inland from the city. "Is it navigable?"

The captain leaned over from the controls and looked at the chart. "That's the St. John River." He nodded. "Yes, it's very navigable, once you get past the reversing falls."

"Reversing falls?"

"That's what they're called." Phillipe grinned. "You see, the Bay of Fundy has an enormous tidal range, sometimes as much as forty feet between high and low tides. When it is low tide, the water flowing from the river must drop down to the level of the bay, so the river's entrance becomes like a waterfall and no boats can pass through it. When it's high tide, the water level in the bay rises and the waterfall disappears completely. The water actually begins to flow up the river. It's quite a sight. I will show it to you in the morning."

"So you can only go up the river when it's high tide?" Frank asked.

"Yes, unless you want to carry your boat over the falls." Phillipe chuckled. "You must wait for slack high tide, and even then you only have a few minutes to get past the river's entrance safely before the falls start up again."

"How long ago was the last high tide?"

"About a half hour ago. It won't be high tide again until tomorrow morning."

"Do you think Karu could've caught it in time to make it up the river?"

Phillipe shrugged. "I'd say he timed it perfectly. He could've zoomed right up that river, leaving anyone who tried to follow him stuck at its entrance."

Frank quickly went to tell Joe what he had found out.

"What'll we do now?" Joe asked. "If we can't get past the reversing falls until morning, Karu will be way up the river by then."

Frank rubbed his chin. "True. But at least we know which way he's going. That's more than Karu thinks we know. And we can be sure that he isn't coming back before tomorrow morning. He can't get down the reversing falls any better than we can get up. We'll just have to wait for high tide, when the river starts to flow in the other direction, before—"

Suddenly, both boys stared at each other with the same thought. The Apocalypse cultists had spoken of a river that flowed two ways. At first the notion had seemed absurd, but now it didn't. Being Canadians, they could have meant the St. John!

Frank pulled the map of Canada from his pants pocket and opened it up again. The St. John River ran straight through New Brunswick, cutting across the area where they believed Lafoote had left the train. In fact, the train route crossed right over the river at one point.

"I bet that's Sligo Tressel!" Joe said. "Maybe that's where we'll find both Lafoote and Karu. Maybe even the Devil himself!"

"Up a river that flows both ways," Frank uttered, recalling the strange words of the cult leader. "You will find Satan hiding deep in the forest, building an army of men the size of trees."

"With which he will lay waste to the earth," Joe added, completing the strange prophecy.

12   On the Devil's Trail

"Would you mind taking us up the river in the morning?" Frank asked Phillipe.

"Not at all."

Once in the harbor, they filled up their tanks, then the captain took the boat to the mouth of the St. John River and dropped anchor for the night. It was too dark to see the falls, but Frank and Joe could hear the dull roar of the water as it cascaded down into the harbor.

Before retiring, the boys used the boat's radio and asked the marine telephone operator to connect them with Mr. Chester.

"You're probably right about Karu going up

the St. John River," the agent's voice came thinly over the speaker, once they'd told him the news. "Stay on his trail as long as you can, then call me and I'll take over."

"Roger," Frank said. "We'll be on the river first thing in the morning. May I talk to Dad for a minute?"

A few seconds later, the voice of Fenton Hardy came over the line. "How's it going?" he asked.

"Not bad, Dad. But we'll need your help."

"You've got it."

"Good. Could you get on the train that runs from Montreal through New Brunswick? Go to a flag stop called Sligo Tressel. It should be a bridge over the St. John River. When you get there, stand on top of the tressel, and if you see us coming up the river, give a shout."

"Sure," the famous detective said in a puzzled tone. "But why such a strange assignment?"

"I'll explain later," Frank answered. "We think your case could tie in with the camper who was kidnapped. We need you at the bridge so we'll know when we've reached it."

"Okay. Is that all?"

"Not quite. Could you bring disguises for Joe and me? We want to look like lumberjacks in search of work. See if you can dig up old dungarees, boots, and a couple of wigs."

"Right. I'll see you tomorrow. I ought to make it to Sligo Tressel by midafternoon."

"If we're not there by nightfall, take the next train back," Frank stated. "But if it works out right, we'll be seeing you there."

After signing off, the boys curled up in sleeping bags on the cabin floor. Then, at the first light of dawn, they were up again and pulled in the lobster boat's anchor. The sound of cascading water was gone, and, as the tide rose higher, the turbulence at the mouth of the river began to smooth out. An hour later, the reversing falls were totally calm.

"Let's go!" Phillipe called out as he throttled the engines up. "We only have a few minutes!"

They plowed through the water and up the river. When they rounded the first bend, they saw Candir Karu's boat coming full steam in the other direction!

"What should we do?" Phillipe cried. "Do you want to turn around?"

Frank and Joe stooped behind the gunwale and watched the fishing vessel chug by on its way over the reversing falls. The agent didn't appear to be aboard, only the two crewmen they had seen before.

"No," Frank instructed at last. "Karu was

probably dropped off somewhere. Keep going."

Staying on course, Phillipe went up the St. John River. It snaked through rolling farmlands and stretches of forest, and by the time the sun hung directly overhead, the boat had passed beneath several train tressels. It wasn't until two o'clock that the youths spotted a lone figure standing in the middle of a railroad bridge waving at them.

"It's Dad!" Joe exclaimed, waving back.

Phillipe swung to shore below the tressel. "Do you want me to wait for you?" he asked his passengers.

"No, thanks, Phillipe." Frank smiled and shook the captain's hand. "You've been a great help, but you'd be too conspicuous just sitting in the water waiting for us. Besides, we may be here a couple of days."

Phillipe wished the boys luck, and after they'd stepped ashore, he turned down the river. Frank and Joe climbed up the bank to the train tracks and scanned the terrain to either side of them. Except for several small farms along the river, dense forest covered the area as far as the eye could see. The faint line of a mountain range cut into the sky on the horizon.

"Well, I brought the disguises you asked for," Mr. Hardy greeted his sons when they walked up to him. "Now would you mind explaining what this is all about?"

"It's just a hunch, Dad," Frank replied. "When Mr. Chester mentioned the foreign country's plan to develop superathletes, I couldn't help thinking about the camper we just saved from being kidnapped. His parents are both top-notch athletes—a football star and an Olympic speed skater—and the boy is already a champion swimmer himself."

"So you think his kidnapping might have something to do with the genetic engineering scheme," Mr. Hardy said, keenly interested in his son's theory.

Frank nodded and explained about the story of the Devil in the northern forest, the army of giants, and the river that ran two ways. He also told about the old man at the train depot, who believed the descendants of the legendary giant, Paul Bunyan, were still living deep in the woods.

"When we put it all together, we knew something strange was going on up here," Joe said. "But we didn't know what it was. All we had was a bunch of weird stories and the fact that Lafoote was taking the kidnapped camper to Sligo Tressel."

"Then, when we followed Karu to the reversing falls at the mouth of the St. John River, it hit us," Frank added. "He was going right up the same river the Devil supposedly inhabits, and the one that Sligo Tressel crosses!"

"The Devil may be the genetic engineer, Randolph Rhee," Mr. Hardy completed his son's thought. "Lafoote may have been on his way there with George Watley so Dr. Rhee could use him in his research."

Frank nodded. "Anyway, we'll try to pick up Lafoote's trail again and see if he leads us to Karu and possibly to Rhee."

For a few seconds nobody spoke. What if Randolph Rhee, the famed genetic scientist, had really managed to assemble an army of supermen over the past ten years, an army of mindless giants who obeyed his every command!

"Be extremely careful," Fenton Hardy finally said. "It takes a nasty guy to build up a reputation as Satan, even if he's mortal like the rest of us. I wish I could go with you, but I'm afraid I'd blow your cover and make this more risky than it already is. No one would believe *I* was a lumberjack."

"Don't worry, Dad," Joe said with a sparkle in his eyes. "We'll do our nosy-kid routine and they won't suspect a thing. Karu thinks he lost us and Lafoote doesn't even know we're on his trail."

"Okay. But if you meet up with any trouble, try to call. Mr. Chester can have his federal agents here within a few hours. We'll be waiting to hear from you."

Fenton Hardy handed Frank and Joe the disguises they'd asked for: hiking boots, work shirts, old jeans, and hats. He also supplied them with wigs made of short black hair, special contact lenses to alter their eye colors, and fake Canadian identification papers under the names Chris and Barney Fadden. By the time the brothers had dressed, they were unrecognizable.

"I saw several lumberjacks get off the train at the other end of the tressel," the detective said in parting. "There's a dirt road down that way."

"Thanks, Dad." Frank grinned. "We'll keep you posted."

Looking like two roughneck backwoods kids, the brothers left their father on the tressel waiting for the next train back. They hiked down the dirt road through the forest for almost five miles before they came to their first logging camp. It was a small operation, with one main building for cutting and storing timber. Among the lumberjacks milling about they saw no one they recognized from the Vermont contest.

"We're looking for work," Frank said to a man who carried a clipboard under his arm. "Are you hiring?" He was careful to conceal his American accent behind a drawling Scottish burr. Though French-Canadians made up the majority of the region's inhabitants, others were of Scottish or Irish descent.

"No work here," the man said brusquely, hardly giving the youths a glance. "Try up the road another ten miles at Peapack. They always need help, but they don't pay much."

The boys thanked the man and asked for a drink of water before starting their trek.

"Go ahead. Water's in the pump around back."

Frank and Joe loitered around the camp just long enough to make sure neither Lafoote nor Karu was there before starting off down the dirt road again. By the time they reached the Peapack Lumber Company, it was evening, and they were exhausted. But they were hired, and signed up under their phony names, Chris and Barney Fadden.

"You get twenty dollars a day, plus room and board," a wiry office manager mumbled through a fat cigar planted in a corner of his mouth. "There are extra bunks in shed number four.

Dinner is in the building next to shed number two."

The lumber camp resembled an army barracks, but instead of guns and artillery, there were axes and cross-cut saws leaning against the walls of the unpainted wooden sheds. Machines for grappling and hoisting logs were also part of the scene; they now stood idle near piles of felled trees.

"Where is everyone?" Joe muttered as they surveyed the grounds.

"Probably at dinner," Frank said. "Come on, let's join them."

The dining hall was filled with long rows of wooden tables and benches. Karu and Lafoote were not there, and the lumberjacks, muddied and hungry from the day's work, hardly looked up from their plates when the young strangers entered and sat down. Not, that is, until Joe asked one of them to pass the stew.

"You kids are pretty young to be lumbering," a man with a scraggly black beard and a hooked nose said in a thick French accent. "This is man's work."

"We can pull our weight," Joe declared, taking the bowl of stew and laddling some out on his plate.

"Where you boys from?" the man prodded.

123

"Halifax," Frank said tersely, giving his voice a Scottish lilt. "We heard there was work up this way. Been on the road a long time."

"How long is this road, anyhow?" Joe asked, hungrily gulping down the stew as if it were delicious, when in fact it tasted like boiled shoes. "Seems we've been on it forever."

The hooked-nosed man cracked a thin smile. "This road's been around since the days when lumber was big in these parts, back when ships were made of wood and lots of timber was needed to build 'em. You could walk north for a week and still not come to the end. It goes into the mountains, and I don't know where it stops."

"Are there any more lumber camps up that way?" Frank inquired. "Maybe we can find a place with better wages."

"Only one or two," the man replied. "Most of 'em are shut down, and the ones that ain't don't pay no more than here anyhow. This is the best you're gonna do."

Frank took a deep breath and steadied his nerves. "Maybe that's because Paul Bunyan's kinfolk are getting all the good timber!" He laughed, trying to make his remark sound jovial. "I heard they were all living in the country to the north."

Suddenly, a hush fell over the table and the loggers stopped eating to glare at the young strangers. Frank and Joe felt the blood drain from their faces as a few of the men began to clutch table knives tightly in their fists!

13 *Bunyans and Bunions*

"Wha-wha . . . what's wrong?" Frank stammered nervously. "It was just a joke."

"Who told you about Bunyan's kinfolk?" the hook-nosed lumberjack asked coldly.

The brothers looked around at the workers, who were still holding their knives in a threatening way.

"We heard it from a man at a train depot," Joe said honestly. "He was just a crazy old guy full of wild stories. We didn't believe a word he said."

The lumberjack looked at the others, who now relaxed their grips on the knives. "Must've been old Luke. He doesn't know how to keep his mouth shut."

The men grunted and went back to eating their stew, and the Hardys breathed inward sighs of relief.

"What did you get so upset about?" Frank decided to ask, knowing it would seem odd if he didn't continue to play dumb.

"Never you mind," the lumberjack warned. "Just forget about what that old man told you. And don't start asking a bunch of fool questions. It might not be good for your health. Understand?"

Both boys nodded and resumed eating, but their minds were working overtime. When the meal was over they left the dining hall and ambled toward the sleeping shed they'd been assigned to, waiting until they were out of anyone's earshot before daring to speak.

"Those fellows were pretty touchy." Joe shivered at the thought of their near disaster.

Frank shrugged. "I guess I opened my big mouth too soon. But it proves we're on the right track with our Bunyan theory. We'll have to play it straight for a day or two, though. One wrong move and they'll be all over us."

Yet the men had seemed almost as scared as

they had been ferocious, and the boys were itching to hike up the road into the mountains. It was as if some evil power had a grasp over the whole region, a power the lumberjacks both feared and protected.

After bunking down for the night, Frank and Joe were up and at work early next morning loading logs on a truck. They kept busy and said nothing, trying to allay any suspicions that might still linger in the lumberjacks' minds. All went well until they'd finished lunch and were positioning the huge timbers at the foot of the hauling truck.

"Watch out!" Joe cried suddenly.

The steel hooks on the crane that hoisted the logs on the truck had released their load too early, dropping the timber onto the truck with a loud crash. A split second later, the whole pile was rolling off the vehicle!

Frank and Joe dove headlong under the truck, just missing being crushed beneath the weight of the tumbling wood!

"Phew!" Joe gasped. "That was too close for comfort!"

"Joe! Your wig!" Frank exclaimed.

Although they'd anchored the black-haired wigs to their heads with special pins, Joe's had come lose when he'd hit the ground, exposing his blond hair underneath. He quickly adjusted his disguise and looked around to see if anyone had noticed, but the crane operator was the only other person nearby and he appeared to be busy working his controls.

"I'm glad nobody saw that!" Joe whispered anxiously. "It would've been curtains for us!"

"It would've been curtains if those logs had hit us, too," Frank added, eyeing the crane operator suspiciously.

He was a balding man in a T-shirt, who now stuck his head through the window. "Are you kids okay?" he called out. "Sorry, I guess I let those logs go too soon! It happens sometimes!"

"We're all right!" Frank returned. "No thanks to you," he added under his breath, as he forced a smile.

Just then, Joe's eye caught a fleeting glimpse of a face in the kitchen window. "Uh-oh," he gulped. "We're not out of the woods yet. I think one of the cooks was watching this whole show."

Making up a hasty excuse to the crane operator about having to clean some minor wounds, the brothers hurried to the kitchen. If the cook had seen Joe lose his wig, their only hope was to convince him not to tell anyone.

To their surprise, the man was as eager to see them as they were to see him. He was a short, roly-poly Frenchman with a handlebar mustache.

"Boys! Boys!" he chirped in a high-pitched, nervous voice, urging the Hardys into the kitchen and shutting the door. "I'm happy you came. I was going to talk to you later, but I was afraid they would see me."

"Who? The lumberjacks?" Joe asked, baffled.

"Yes. I heard them talking last night after you left dinner. One of them's going up to Mr. Bunyan's camp today to get instructions, then they'll all be back to ask you questions. You'll be in big trouble!"

"Did you see what happened just now?" Frank took over, deciding to trust the man.

"How could I not see?" the little French cook replied, raising his eyebrows and turning his palms up. "I think that man dropped the logs on purpose. Maybe they won't even wait until they get the word to . . ." The cook finished the sentence by drawing his finger across his throat like a knife.

"Who *is* this Paul Bunyan character?" Joe queried. "You don't actually believe he's the son of the legendary giant lumberjack, do you?"

"I have never seen him myself, if that's what you mean," the cook replied. "But I have seen the footprints of Paul Bunyan, Junior, and they are as big as a bed! You know, the first Bunyan was said to live up in Madawaska, which is not far from here. So it's not hard to believe that his descendants still roam these forests!"

Madawaska, the Hardys had noticed when studying the map of New Brunswick, was an area to the north that was once a separate province before becoming a part of New Brunswick.

"Why are the people here protecting him so?" Frank asked. "Are they afraid of him? Does he have some kind of hold over them?"

"Paul Bunyan, Junior is not at all like his father, God rest his soul." The French cook frowned. "He is a cruel man, and he won't let anyone close to him or his family—except the few chosen men he has employed to do his devilish work."

"What sort of devilish work?"

"I don't know. There are a couple of men here at the camp who know Bunyan. They are the ones who are dangerous to you. But as far as I know, they are merely guards—or spies, if you like. Their job is simply to warn and protect. I know no more than that. They are not very sociable or friendly men."

"And you don't know where Bunyan's camp is?" Joe inquired.

The cook shook his head. "Only that he lives north of here."

"How long ago did this Paul Bunyan, Junior appear in these parts?" Frank posed one last question.

"Oh, let's see," the man said, losing himself in thought as he gazed out the window. "It must be close to ten years since I first heard of him. I didn't believe he really existed at first, but over the years I became certain that it was true."

The brothers glanced at each other. It had been ten years since the NIH genetic engineering project had been ended and Randolph Rhee had disappeared.

"Thanks for your help." Frank smiled. "We'd better be going. Those guys may come back at any time."

"Please don't tell anyone I warned you," the little cook urged. "I've taken a great risk, but I couldn't just stand by and let two fine young boys like you be . . ." Again he drew his finger across his throat.

"Can we sneak out a back door?" Joe asked, convinced now that the crane operator had dropped the timber on purpose.

"Yes. I'll show you the way. But you must

leave quickly and never come back."

Before seeing the Hardys out, the cook offered them some leftover stew for their trip. Both declined politely, remembering its awful taste. But they did stuff their pockets with cheese and apples and took a jar of water before slipping out the door and into the forest.

"Where to now?" Joe wondered aloud. "We can't just march up that road in full view of anyone coming down it."

"No. But we can follow the road under cover of the woods," the older boy replied. "Let's hustle!"

Trudging through the forest alongside the old logging road, the brothers hiked northward. They had enough food to last them for a day or two, but they were without either a tent or sleeping bags. The nights would be cold. Whenever they saw lumberjacks coming down the road hauling newly cut trees behind tractors, they ducked into the underbrush and waited for the men to pass before starting on their way again. By early evening, the boys' feet were aching.

"Let's stop here." Joe sighed, leaning on a tree. "My feet are killing me. I think I have a corn on my heel. Or maybe it's a bunion," he quipped.

Frank groaned at the joke. Then he said, "Seems as good a spot as any," and sat down with his back against the trunk. "I just hope there aren't any hungry bears prowling around them thar woods tonight!"

Having long ago gotten rid of their disguises, the boys huddled together at the base of the tree, warding off the chilly evening air as best they could. Soon they were both dozing peacefully.

CRACK!!!

Frank's eyes blinked open at the sharp sound of something hitting the tree. The early-morning sunlight was filtering through the forest, and he looked up to see an ax embedded squarely in the trunk above his head! He blinked again and focused on a group of grizzly men standing around him with malicious leers on their faces! In the center of the group was Pierre Lafoote!

"Joe!" Frank cried, nudging his sleeping brother. "Wake up!"

14 Logger's Revenge

Joe came to his senses as Pierre Lafoote stepped forward and yanked the ax out of the tree. His dark beady eyes glared ferociously above his bushy black beard.

"Good morning," he sneered. "I am so glad we meet again. I hope you will enjoy the little game I have arranged for you."

"G-g-game?" Joe sputtered, realizing that they were far too outnumbered to escape.

The man's lips curled up in a fiendish grin. "Yes, a game—just like the contest your friends enjoyed so much in Vermont. Only this time you will not only play lumberjacks, you will also be the lumber!"

The men howled with laughter as Lafoote sank his ax into the tree once more. Then they jerked the brothers off the ground and bound their hands behind their backs with rope.

"How did you find us?" Frank asked, as he and Joe were pushed into the forest.

"It was nothing." Lafoote shrugged. "I have tracked wild animals through the woods—sometimes for days. You were easy."

"You can't make us talk!" Joe spat.

"I don't expect you to talk, my boy. I expect you to die!"

Lafoote emitted a cruel laugh as he watched his captives' faces grow pale with dread.

"The police know exactly where we are," Frank said, trying to keep his voice steady. "If they don't hear from us very soon, they will close in on this whole area. They know all about Paul Bunyan, Junior and what he is doing."

Lafoote stopped in his tracks. "You are lying!" he snarled.

"Oh, yes? Then maybe you don't care to hear what we know about Candir Karu and Randolph Rhee!"

Frank had played his only trump card. Either the names Rhee or Karu meant something to the lumberjack or the boys had made the wrong deduction.

The man's face went blank for a fraction of a second, then he glared hostilely at his young prisoner. "What do you know about them?" he snapped.

Frank shrugged. "No more than the feds do! And they're right behind us!"

"If you two really knew what was going on here, you wouldn't have dared to come!" Lafoote spoke with a hint of doubt in his voice. "And if the feds, as you call them, knew what was going on, they would've been here long ago!"

"Believe what you want!" Joe put in. "But then, you can't be sure, can you, Mr. Lafoote?"

"Soon I will be sure. It will just make our game a little more . . . interesting."

After a short march, the group arrived at the edge of a narrow, winding river. It was much smaller than the St. John, and the boys assumed it was one of its minor tributaries.

"This is the beginning of my game," Lafoote announced, pointing at several logs floating near the bank. "Remember the log-rolling contest in Vermont? Now you will have a chance to try it, too, just like your friends. There will only be one difference—your hands will be tied."

With ax blades at their backs, the Hardys were

forced to mount one of the pieces of timber. The men climbed on other logs around them, getting ready to enjoy the sport.

"You won't get away with this!" Frank warned one last time, hoping some of the lumberjacks would lose their nerve.

"You are the ones who won't get away!" Lafoote bellowed. "Now start rolling."

The brothers were prodded to their feet at either end of the log. Gingerly they tried to set it in motion without falling off. But they knew it was hopeless. With their hands tied behind their backs, it was impossible to keep their balance. They splashed into the water a moment later.

The evil Canadian laughed uproariously as he watched the Hardys struggle to stay afloat. He waited until they started to sink, gasping and choking for air, then he ordered his men to fish them out.

"Now are you ready to talk?" he demanded.

Frank spat out some water and shook his head. He knew they were doomed whether they told Lafoote anything or not.

"Then we'll try something else!" Lafoote shouted. He turned to the loggers. "Take them down to the sawmill!"

Still sputtering and coughing, the boys were

led along the riverbank until they came to an old wooden building. It was rotted and listing to one side, reminding the Hardys of the barn the Apocalypse cult used for its rituals.

One of the men opened the door and the young detectives were shoved inside.

"Oh, no!" Joe shuddered when he saw that the building contained a huge circular saw. It was easily six feet in diameter and, powered by a gasoline-driven generator in the corner, could cut through giant logs as easily as if they were sticks of butter.

"You're not really going to . . ." Frank gasped, feeling weak in the knees.

"Ah, but I *am*," Lafoote replied. "As I told you before, you will now be the lumber in our little game!"

His eyes lit up like a madman's as he grabbed Frank and lifted him up on a long wooden conveyer track that was used to draw logs underneath the saw's enormous blade. With the help of one of the men, he tied the boy securely onto the track.

"Your brother can watch!" Lafoote grinned, looking at Joe. "I'm sure he'll be ready to talk when he sees what'll happen!"

Helpless rage surged through Joe. In desperation, he hurled himself at Lafoote, but the man stepped nimbly out of his way, and the boy, with his hands tied behind his back, crashed to the floor.

"Jacques, tie him to that post over there!" Lafoote hissed, and jerked Joe up by his shoulders.

A light-haired fellow in his thirties stepped foward and took the hapless youth by the arm. He led him to an iron column and tied Joe's wrists to the post. In doing so, however, he loosened the young detective's bonds a little. Joe was sure Jacques did it on purpose and tried to catch the man's eyes. But the lumberjack quickly moved away when he was finished, and confronted his boss.

"I did as you said," he declared. "But I have no stomach to watch what comes next." With that, he walked out the door. All the others followed, and a moment later, Lafoote was alone with his two captives.

"Cowards!" he murmured. "Weaklings. Well, I don't need anyone else now." He glared at Frank. "Are you ready to talk?"

Frozen with fear, Frank glanced at Joe. Almost unnoticeably, Joe shook his head.

"I don't know anything," Frank muttered.

"Well, then the game is over!" Lafoote yelled. He walked over to a control panel to turn on the huge circular saw.

Joe had feverishly worked on his bonds and managed to slip out of them just as the cruel lumberjack reached for the power switch. With a scream, the young detective flew across the room and landed a flying tackle on Lafoote's back.

"Yuuuummmphhh!" the man uttered and slumped to the floor.

15 Hunted Hunters

Joe's shoulder caught the lumberjack right below the ribs, knocking him to the floor with a muffled yelp of pain. The next instant, the blond boy rendered Lafoote unconscious with a sharp jab to the jaw.

Frank had watched the scene with relief.

"Great job, Joe. Now get me off this contraption!" he urged his brother.

Using Lafoote's razor-sharp ax, Joe cut the ropes, and soon Frank was on his feet. "Good grief," the older Hardy said with a sigh as he wiped the sweat from his forehead. "Remind me that I owe you a favor real soon!"

"What'll we do with him?" Joe whispered frantically, knowing that the other lumberjacks were waiting just outside the building.

"Nothing. Let's get out of here pronto. Those guys will be back in a flash if they think something's wrong."

Leaving Pierre Lafoote's crumpled body on the floor, Frank and Joe climbed out a back window and darted into the forest without looking back. Shortly, they could hear shouts of alarm ring out behind them, and they knew the lumberjacks would soon be hot on their trail again.

Both top sprinters on their high school track team, the Hardys flew among the banks of the wide brook, putting as much distance between themselves and the lumberjacks as possible before stopping to rest.

"We have to outfox those bullies," Joe panted. "We can't run like this all day!"

"I know!" Frank puffed, then quickly outlined his plan to avoid being recaptured. It was simple, if somewhat risky. Joe agreed wholeheartedly.

"Okay, let's get going," he said. "Lafoote and his logging gang can't be far behind."

To obscure their trail, the boys crossed and recrossed the brook several times. This would

144

confuse Lafoote enough to keep him busy for a while, but coming from a heritage of expert French-Canadian trappers, he would no doubt pick up their trail eventually.

"Now we start our fancy footwork," Frank stated. "If this doesn't do the trick, nothing will."

The boys turned around and zigzagged back upstream, cutting across the trail they'd already made and crossing the brook in such a way that Lafoote wouldn't be able to tell which trail was which. Then they waded along in the water and hid in an outcropping of rocks along the bank. It wasn't long before they spotted the lumberjacks half a mile upstream, sloshing through the water for the spot where the trail picked up again.

"Here it is!" one of them called out, finding footprints in the mud.

"No!" another yelled. "I found it over here!"

Soon, the lumberjacks were in a state of confusion as to where one trail left off and another began. The brothers heard Lafoote cursing. He knew he'd been duped.

"Forget it!" he shouted angrily. "Those punks have used a trick I know well. We'll be all day trying to find the right trail!"

His reaction was exactly what the Hardys had hoped for. He gave up his search and marched his men off into the woods.

"Now it's *our* turn to do a bit of tracking," Frank declared, gazing after the men.

When the lumberjacks had disappeared, the sleuths left their hiding place and followed the group's footprints. A while later, they found themselves once again on the logging road, where the marks ended and were replaced by tire tracks in the dirt.

"This is it," Joe said, gauging the size of the tread marks. "A truck must've been waiting here to pick them up. Lafoote's probably on his way to warn his boss."

"Maybe we should call our agent, Mr. Chester, and have him take over," Frank said, feeling discouraged. "Our covers are blown, it seems like half of Canada's population wants to do us in, and now Bunyan, Rhee, the Devil, or whoever he is, will be ready for us. If we could just find a phone, we could —" Suddenly his eye caught sight of something and he stooped down.

One set of bootprints led away from the others and continued in the opposite direction!

"Joe! Someone didn't get on that truck!" the boy called excitedly.

146

Joe looked down the road with renewed hopes. "Do you think it was Lafoote?"

"I don't know. But whoever it was, we may have a chance to catch him alone."

Breaking into a jog, the Hardys followed the prints, finally catching sight of a lone figure ahead of them. It was not Lafoote, but from the man's red-and-black-patched jacket, they could tell he was one of the lumberjacks who had captured them.

"Circle around and distract him," Frank ordered in a whisper. "I'll jump him from the rear."

Joe went off through the trees, stepping into the road again forty yards in front of the man, while Frank crept up from behind. Joe acted as if he were startled by the sight of the lumberjack, turned around, and began to run away. He even beefed up his act by pretending to fall and twist his ankle.

The man, who carried an ax, started after him. A second later, Frank hit him at the knees, bringing him to the ground and knocking the ax out of his hands. In a flash, both boys had him stapled to the ground.

"Please don't hurt me!" the man pleaded. He was younger than the other lumberjacks, with hazel eyes and a pockmarked complexion.

"Don't hurt you, eh?" Joe snapped angrily. "After what you tried to do to us, we should take you back to that sawmill and slice you up into two-by-fours!"

"Lafoote made us do it!" the young logger gagged, his eyes wild with fear. "Please! You don't understand! If we hadn't gone along with the plan, he would've done the same thing to *us*!"

Joe relaxed his grip, recalling that this man hadn't been laughing at the boys' recent log-rolling trial, and had been one of the first to leave the sawmill after Frank was tied to the pulley. He also remembered Jacques, who had loosened his bonds. Apparently some of these henchmen were decent, if passively obedient.

"Then you'd better start to explain things," the blond youth declared, "and tell us all you know!"

"I will! I will!" the hazel-eyed lumberjack sputtered.

The Hardys learned that Paul Bunyan, Jr. was indeed alive and very real. "Pierre Lafoote is one of Bunyan's henchmen who do his dirty work while the giant stays hidden in the north with his family," the young man reported. "All

148

the lumberjacks live in constant fear of Bunyan. If they do his bidding, they are left alone and rewarded handsomely for their service. But if they dare to cross him or spread word of him, they are dealt with cruelly."

"Have you ever *seen* this giant?" Frank queried.

The frightened man shook his head. "Most of us haven't. He gives his orders through Lafoote and a handful of other men. They are the only ones allowed near him."

"Tell us where he lives!" Joe demanded, growing impatient with the feeble account of Bunyan, which wasn't much more than what the cook had already told them.

"I don't know. It's a secret."

"That's not good enough." Joe glared at him. "You're going to the sawmill. Maybe the menacing sound of that saw will sharpen your memory!"

The Hardys pulled the man up and lashed his hands together with his belt. Then they prodded the man into the forest. With each step, the lumberjack grew more apprehensive, and by the time they came to the brook, his knees were shaking.

"Okay, okay," he said nervously. "You win. I'll

149

tell you all I know. But later on you'll wish I'd never opened my mouth."

"We'll be the judges of that," Frank said. "Now talk. And it had better be the truth!"

"Bunyan's camp is called the Demon's Den. It's up the logging road about fifteen miles. There, another road forks off to the left and winds around the mountain. It's marked by some tree stumps—and that's all I know."

"And the Demon's Den is down that road?"

"Yes."

"Is that where Lafoote has gone?"

The lumberjack nodded. "He was going to warn Bunyan about you boys after dropping off the other men."

"Fine. Then you can take us there," Frank declared.

"*Take* you there?" the hostage cried in disbelief. "You're crazy! Lafoote is a pygmy compared to Bunyan! That giant could tear us apart with his bare hands!"

"You only have to take us as far as the fork," Frank promised. "Now let's get moving."

Reluctantly, the man obeyed. "You kids have no idea what's up there," he said. "It's not only Bunyan himself; I've heard he has ten sons of his own, all just as nasty as he is."

Neither boy believed the story about the giant and his cruel sons, but as they headed north toward the mountains, they were less than happy at the thought of what they might encounter. Instead of risking being seen on the road, they followed the bubbling brook to the foot of the mountain range. The peaks loomed above them, majestic and beautiful, but there was also something dark and mysterious about them.

"There's still time to turn back," the lumberjack warned. "If you untie me, I'll see that you get safely out of New Brunswick and away from these dreadful giants."

"No way," Joe said, trying to sound determined. "The only giants around here are those huge mountains."

Their captive shrugged. "You're about to find out how wrong you are," he murmured. "And then it'll be too late."

16 Zombies

On foot, the threesome rounded the base of one mountain, planning to intersect the logging road as it entered the range. It wasn't long, though, before they stumbled on something that made them reconsider their plans.

A huge bootprint was set deeply in the ground, having flattened a small bush. "Wow!" Joe gulped, staring down at the enormous print. "This looks like a size twenty-five!"

"Must belong to one of Bunyan's kids," the lumberjack said, judging the dimensions of the bootprint. "He'd be about twelve to fifteen feet tall."

For a moment, Frank was speechless. A short way farther on was another huge print—then another and another—following a course directly up the side of the mountain.

"Forget the road," he uttered at last. "We'll trail these prints."

"Don't tell me you're still planning to go through with this?" the lumberjack quavered.

"We sure are," Frank replied evenly. "And so are you!"

"Oh, no, I'm not! I'm not taking one more foolish step. I don't care what you threaten to do to me!" The frightened man plopped down on the ground, refusing to budge.

Frank sighed. He knew their captive couldn't be reasoned with, and time was too precious to waste.

"What'll we do with him?" Joe asked. "If we leave him here, he'll run back to the others and they'll come after us."

"No, I won't!" The man looked pleadingly at the boys, and there was no hint of deception in his eyes. "I know you have no good reason to trust me but I beg you to take my word. I don't want any more trouble. Please believe me."

"He's right," Frank decided, and untied the lumberjack's wrists. Slowly, their hostage stood up and turned down the mountain. He looked back once more. "Good luck," he murmured feebly. "I hope you live to tell someone your story."

The brothers stood hesitantly, then started through the forest after the giant footsteps.

"I wonder what did make these tracks." Joe frowned as they hiked over ever-higher terrain until the trees began to thin out.

"It's probably just a scare tactic," Frank said, "all part of a camouflage to keep the lumberjacks fearful and obedient."

"Do you think Randolph Rhee really engineered a race of giants over these last ten years?" Joe went on.

Frank shrugged. "We can be sure he made *some* advances, otherwise that foreign country wouldn't have contacted him to produce super-athletes. But I'd be very surprised if he'd managed to create an army of supermen. Even with genetic engineering, life forms have to grow naturally. You can't just put them together like Frankenstein's monster!"

"But take George Watley, who was already over six feet tall at the age of twelve. Maybe by some means of genetic fiddling, that height could be doubled—or even tripled!"

"The mind boggles, doesn't it?" Frank mused. "I've heard of nine-foot giants in circus side shows. Maybe Paul Bunyan, Junior is some sort of freak, and Rhee is using his genes to clone a whole bunch of them. That would explain the myth about Bunyan and his children and the story about the Devil."

"But Dr. Peters said cloning people isn't possible yet," Joe objected, even though he was beginning to feel a bit weak in his knees as he followed the huge bootprints around the mountain.

Suddenly the boys spotted a thin column of smoke rising from a low, narrow valley, and they saw the sun reflecting off the tin roofs of several buildings.

Frank took a deep breath. "There's the Demon's Den!" he exclaimed. "Pretty soon, we'll know what this incredible giant business is all about."

"I'm not sure I want to find out," Joe muttered as he sat against a tree to rest. Frank joined him. But despite their being tired and frightened, the boys were curious enough to be up again in a few minutes. Cautiously, they made their way down into the valley toward the tin-roofed buildings.

"If we were smart, we'd turn around," Joe said. "After all, Mr. Chester only asked us to go as far as we thought would be safe. Even if there *is* no army of giants down there, you can bet Mr. Lafoote is lying in wait for us!"

"Not on your life!" Frank said, determinedly marching on. "I want to get a look-see at this Bunyan character and his family. Anyway, what could we tell Mr. Chester now? We don't even know what's in those buildings. All we have is a hunch that it may be Rhee's operation."

The younger boy smiled. "Just thought I'd give you one more chance to chicken out."

When the Hardys got closer to the buildings, they saw no signs of activity. Three of the structures were long and barrackslike, left over from the days when lumber camps abounded in New Brunswick. They were of average dimensions, with doors for normal-sized people to use. The fourth building to which the huge bootprints led was a big barn with its wide doors closed.

"Plenty of room for giants in there," Joe commented from their vantage point behind a clump of bushes.

"True. And check out that ax!"

Leaning against the barn was an ax. The boys had never seen anything like it. Its handle was as long as a broomstick, and the steel head on it looked as big as a shovel!

"Another scare device," Frank declared.

"And a very clever one." Joe grimaced.

Suddenly, a boy came out of one of the barracks. Like George, he was impressively big for his age, standing over six feet high, though he seemed no older than fourteen or fifteen. But he was no giant.

"Well, that settles one question." Joe sighed with relief. "That Bunyan story's a big hoax. I bet this boy is supposed to be one of Bunyan's kids."

"Hm," Frank agreed, noticing that the lad wore a T-shirt with DELTA printed on it. "That may settle one question, but it raises a whole lot of others!"

Keeping out of sight, he began to shake on a bush limb, creating a rustling sound to attract the youth's attention.

The boy, who'd been toting a knapsack over to a truck, glanced around. As he did, Frank imitated the whimpering sound of an injured dog. The oversized boy set his knapsack on the ground and walked toward the bushes to investigate. When he was close enough, the brothers pounced on him.

"Hey! What's the big idea?" the youth droned angrily as the detectives wrestled him to the ground. "Get off me!"

"We don't want to harm you," Frank explained. "We just want to ask you some questions. Okay?"

The boy, who had curly brown hair and blue eyes, tried to bite Frank's hand, which was cupped over his mouth. At the same time, he struggled violently to free himself of their grasp. It took all of their might to keep him from breaking away.

"Listen, Delta," Frank repeated, narrowly missing having his fingers chomped, "we only want to talk to you for a minute, then we'll let you go. Promise."

The youth relaxed somewhat, and Frank lifted his hand from the boy's mouth. It proved to be a big mistake.

"*Help!!!!*" Delta bellowed, filling the woods with his cry.

The barracks door flew open and three more young, extra-large boys burst out into the sunlight. They wore T-shirts marked ALPHA, BETA, and OMEGA, and they looked anxiously around to see where the cry had come from.

The Hardys tensely held their captive down,

hoping the others would return inside. Just then, a German shepherd bounded from behind the building, heading straight for the clump of bushes and barking all the way. When the dog reached the brothers, it stopped with a fang-baring snarl. Frank and Joe froze, knowing that one move could mean their throats.

"Someone's in the bushes!" one of the boys exclaimed. "Come on!"

In seconds, Frank and Joe were pinned to the ground by four sets of huge hands and legs.

"We will take them to the master," the boy wearing the OMEGA T-shirt ordered in a flat, mechanical voice.

Aside from his immense size and strength, Omega seemed to be a normal teenager. Yet with his robotlike manner and a glazed look in his eyes, he appeared to be in a trance, almost as if he were under hypnosis!

Frank and Joe studied the faces of the others and saw that they all were in the same condition. They had strangely blank expressions, and when they spoke, it was in the same flat monotone.

"They tried to make me answer questions, but I said nothing," Delta declared.

"That is good," Omega replied. "The master will reward you."

The four youths started to lift Frank and Joe to their feet, and the Hardys knew they would have to think fast.

"Can we just talk to you for a minute?" Frank asked in a friendly way. "I mean, wouldn't you like to know who we are and where we came from before you turn us over to your master? We'll do all the talking. You don't have to say anything if you don't want to."

A light flickered in Omega's eyes, and Frank knew he was on the right track. Apparently, behind their trancelike expressions, the boys were eager to hear about the world outside their camp. But then Omega had second thoughts.

"No," he said flatly. "You must go to the master now."

Joe shrugged. "Well, I guess you don't care about things like moon rockets and roller coasters," he said coyly. "Maybe you like football and basketball? You should hear about how we won last year's championship football game for our high school with a forty-yard touchdown pass that . . ." Joe paused. "But if you guys aren't interested, we'll forget it and just go to your master."

By now, the youths' blank faces burned with eagerness to hear the Hardys' stories, and they looked pleadingly at Omega.

161

"The master told us not to talk with any strangers," he warned. "You know we cannot disobey."

"We won't tell on you." Frank smiled assuringly. "Your master will never know. What are you afraid of?"

"I . . . I've never been on a roller coaster!" the youngest one suddenly blurted out, unable to control himself anymore. "Have you?"

His remark seemed to break the invisible barrier that had held the boys back, and even Omega couldn't stop them from flooding the Hardys with questions. He finally broke down himself, overwhelmed with curiosity.

"Come on," he said. "We will go to our quarters. But then we will take you to the master."

17 The Master Speaks

"Why don't we just stay out here?" Frank suggested.

"No. Inside," Omega replied, firmly gripping the young detective's arm.

The brothers had hoped to make a break for the forest when their captors were off guard. But the four strong youths were taking no chances. They formed a ring around the Hardys to obscure them from sight and marched them into the barracks, locking the door behind them. The dog, who had followed them, stayed outside.

Now, with rapt attention, the boys sat on bunks and listened as the two visitors regaled them with stories of roller coasters, rocket ships, their school, and their hometown of Bayport.

Omega and his companions soaked up the tales like sponges soak up water. They were eager to hear more and more. If it had not been for the imminent danger, Frank and Joe would have felt like two counselors telling bedtime stories to their campers.

"What about *you* guys?" Joe asked casually, once he felt he'd gained the youths' trust. "What do you do for fun up here?"

Instantly, the blank looks returned to the boys' faces.

"Not much," Beta volunteered at last. "The master doesn't let us go anywhere. He says it's too dangerous. We stay here and help with the chores."

"Are those your names on your shirts?" Joe queried carefully, not wanting to press too hard at first.

The boys nodded.

"They're pretty strange," Frank said. "How did you get them?"

"The master gave them to us," Alpha replied.

"How did you get here?" Joe pressed further.

But with that question, the youths clammed up. They appeared not to know the answer, and stared at the Hardys uneasily.

Frank and Joe were thinking the same

thought. These youngsters not only had no knowledge of the surrounding world, they seemed to know nothing about who they were and where they came from! Could they have been produced in a laboratory without mothers or fathers, or any family history except what the "master" gave them?

"Who is the master?" Frank asked, keenly watching the group for its reaction. "Is he your father?"

The boys sat on their bunks like zombies, not saying a word. The trust and openness were gone from their faces.

"Please," Frank went on. "If you let us help you, we can show you the real world. You can go to school and meet lots of other boys and girls just like you. If we all leave here together, we'll be able to get away—"

"Stop it!" Omega snapped harshly. "We will take you to the master now!"

Yet behind his fierce manner, the boy seemed to be suffering from a great inner pain. His eyes were edged with tears, as if the young detective had struck a very sensitive nerve.

He grabbed Frank's arm and yanked him to his feet. "Don't say one more thing!" he said angrily. "If you do, I'll hit you! Now let's go!"

"But—" Joe began, when a fist caught him

squarely in the solar plexus, doubling him up in pain.

"I warned you!" the boy blurted. "Now move!"

Half-hunched over, Joe walked out of the barracks with one of the oversized boys on each side of him. The other two escorted Frank toward the big barn.

As the door slowly opened, the Hardys gazed at the giant ax leaning against the building. The boys' throats were dry when they stepped inside. Then they gasped in shock as they were confronted by a bushy black beard and a pair of glaring, beady eyes!

"I knew you'd show up," Pierre Lafoote said, cackling. "Please come in. The master has plans for you."

Frank and Joe felt chills running down their spines at the sight of the grizzly French-Canadian. A hollow feeling gripped Joe's stomach.

"Plans?" he breathed.

"Yes. And consider yourselves lucky. If it were up to me, I'd finish you off right now!"

The Hardys were led deeper into the building, which turned out to house a maze of microscopes, test tubes, and papers. It was a laboratory, much like the one they had seen at the Vermont Biological Research Center!

"The master will be with you shortly," Lafoote hissed, erupting into his fiendish laugh. "Make yourselves comfortable, won't you?" He pushed the boys onto stools, and three more lumberjacks joined him to stand guard over the intruders. Then Omega and his companions were ordered to leave the barn.

"You have been very clever," Lafoote said to the Hardys when the boys had disappeared. "Yes, very clever and very brave. I greatly admire the way you tracked me down and set that Watley boy free right under my nose."

"Oh, sure." Frank winced, not even looking at the man. "You admired us so much you were going to saw us into boards."

The French-Canadian's eyes glimmered. "I wasn't going to let you die," he said, stroking his jaw, which Joe's fist had bruised in the sawmill. "I would've stopped the saw in time. You just beat me to the punch, so to speak. You see, the master has *other* plans for you."

"Then why did you go through all that?" Frank asked.

"It would have been a good way to make you talk." Lafoote smiled evilly.

"Why is your master so interested in us?" Joe took over.

Lafoote's smile grew wider. "Because he ad-

167

mires you, too. He thinks you are very good specimens for his experiments. After he lost George, he was upset. But now he is very happy. He will get two for one."

Just then, footsteps could be heard descending a staircase from the barn's upper level. The Hardys tried to stay calm, but the palms of their hands and their foreheads glistened with nervous perspiration, especially since they had now noticed something else that scared them. At the far end of the laboratory was what looked like a fully equipped hospital operating table!

"We might end up diced and quartered yet," Frank whispered, his eyes on an array of surgical implements.

Joe gulped. Perhaps the "master" was planning to perform brain surgery on them and leave them as blank-faced as the other youths, with no identity—no longer Frank and Joe Hardy, but obedient drones with letters of the Greek alphabet for names!

"Hello, boys," a measured voice called out from the stairs. "I see you've come to join our little . . . family."

The Hardys blinked at the sight of a withered man in a white smock, who came toward them at a brisk pace. He had unkempt gray hair and pallid skin, which stretched so tightly over his bones that he looked like a walking skeleton.

"No need for introductions." He grinned. "I know who you are, and from what I understand, you know about me, too."

"Yes, Mr. Rhee," Frank said. "And believe me, the United States government also knows about you and your plans."

"I realize all that." The mad scientist shrugged as if he weren't bothered by the news. "I've been expecting this for years, and I'm way ahead of them. I just wanted to wait for you two to show up before we took off."

"Took off?"

"We have a boat waiting right now, and should be safely out of the country by morning. Have you boys ever been to Greenland?"

"Is Greenland the country that hired you to produce those superathletes?" Frank queried.

Rhee shook his head. "No. It'll only be another hiding place for us. I don't want any more governments meddling in my work, and Greenland's big enough to get lost in."

The Hardys knew about the huge island way up north, which was only populated at its southern tip. The rest of it was a frozen wasteland of mountains. If Rhee managed to make it there, he'd never be found again. Nor would they!

"What are you planning to do with us?" Joe inquired. "Take us with you?"

"Of course. But first I want both of you to be good boys and roll up your sleeves." Rhee opened a drawer and pulled out a syringe, which he filled with a clear fluid.

Frank and Joe leaped up from their stools and bolted for the door, knocking down two of the lumberjacks on their way. But the barn had been padlocked and soon Lafoote and his men had the boys at bay once again.

"Tsk, tsk," Rhee said, wagging his finger as the captives were dragged back to the center of the laboratory. "We mustn't be squeamish, now. You can take a little shot in the arm, can't you? I'll give you a lollipop if you don't cry."

"Very funny!" Joe snapped, seething with anger. "You try knocking us out and they'll put you in jail forever!"

Both Rhee and Lafoote laughed with glee.

"If the authorities ever found me, they'd put me in jail forever anyway." The gray-haired man cackled. "You're just two more drops in the bucket. Now be good boys and hold still."

The guards pinned Joe to the wall while Randolph Rhee stuck the hypodermic needle deeply into his arm and injected the fluid. In moments, the blond boy slumped to the floor.

"Is that the same stuff you used to sedate George?" Frank asked when he, too, was pushed against the wall.

"Yes, it is. And it should keep you both quiet for a long time."

Frank felt the sharp jab of the needle in his own arm. His mind grew fuzzy and he crumpled to the floor next to his brother. The last thing he heard before losing consciousness was Lafoote's voice.

"When you're finished with these two, I'll put 'em in the truck. We should be out of here by nightfall."

18 A Dark Ride

When Frank and Joe finally came to, they found themselves firmly secured with rope in the cargo hold of a large truck. It was enclosed by a broad canvas tarpaulin, preventing the boys from seeing the road. But from the way they bounced, and because no light came through the grommet holes in the canvas, they could tell they were traveling along a rough road in darkness.

"I'm Frank Hardy. I live in Bayport. I'm in Canada with my brother, Joe," Frank muttered quietly to himself, pleased to know he hadn't been surgically transformed into a zombie while unconscious.

Joe had also put his brain through a short exercise to make sure his mind was his own.

"Everything seems to be in working order." The blond boy sighed. "I was afraid we'd be robots like those kids when we woke up. Now we just have to find a way to get out of this mess."

"You won't," a foreign-accented voice spoke sharply from across the cargo hold.

Since the truck was crammed with an assortment of boxes, duffel bags, and scientific gear, the Hardys had not noticed they weren't alone. Now, in the dim light of an oil lamp, they could make out the face of a man with a thin mustache.

"Karu," Joe breathed in recognition.

"Yes," the foreign agent hissed. "And you are my nosy shadows. I should have eliminated you two in Halifax when I had the chance."

The Hardys looked at Candir Karu without speaking, wishing they could get their hands on him for just one minute. Then they scanned the cargo hold, their eyes finally resting on three young boys huddled in the corner. They were Omega, Beta, and Alpha, and they stared at Frank and Joe with half-blank, half-pained expressions.

Frank's face flushed when he realized that the youngsters had probably heard Joe's comment

173

about them. He felt sorry for them and wanted to apologize. But more than that, he was concocting a plan in his head—a plan that might get the boys on his side.

"Follow me," he whispered to Joe. Then he rolled over on his stomach and started to rock with the motion of the truck as it bounced through the night. Though their hands and feet were tightly bound, Frank and Joe were able to wriggle like snakes across the truck's floor.

"Hey!" Karu shouted suddenly. "Where do you think you're going?"

"Just paying a visit," Frank shot back with an annoyed look. "Relax, pal. We can't escape with these ropes around us."

Karu grunted but didn't attempt to stop the boys as they squirmed over to the corner. Soon they were sitting with their backs propped against the truck wall alongside the three boys.

"Hi." Joe smiled. "Would you like to hear some more stories?"

The youngsters nodded in unison. Behind their vacant eyes, a weak flame seemed to flicker again, just as it had earlier at the barracks. Frank was hoping he could kindle that flame to a roaring fire. If only he had enough time!

Alpha, Beta, and Omega listened intently as

174

the Hardys again told them all about their active family and Bayport—their attractive, understanding mother, their kind but feisty Aunt Gertrude, their famous detective father, their yellow sports sedan, their boat, their friends, their school courses, and their sports teams. The young detectives chattered about everything in colorful detail to spark the youths' interest and longing for a happy, normal life of their own.

To cap it off, Joe described one of their recent mysteries, *Sky Sabotage*, in which the sleuths had almost single-handedly stopped the theft of a space satellite at Cape Canaveral.

"Wow!" Alpha exclaimed. "Did you guys really do all that?"

"I wish *I* could go to high school." Beta sighed, knitting his brow. "And I wish I could be a detective, just like you."

Joe glanced at his brother, knowing it was time again to ask the boys about their own lives. If they did open up, it could mean escape for all of them.

"If you'll help us, you *can* do those things," Frank urged. "We'll take you home to Bayport with us and you can go to school, play football, go to parties, and solve mysteries—just like us.

You'd like our mom and dad," Frank added as a final enticement.

"What's a mom and dad?" Omega asked, his face starting to cloud up again. "Are they like the master?"

Frank hesitated for a moment before answering. "Yes, in a way they are like your master," he said at last. "But they are much nicer. They let you have fun and go places on your own. They give you advice and really care about you."

Omega's eyes suddenly became strangely wide and he appeared to sink into a deep trance as he stared off in space. He seemed to be struggling with some inner thought, something he'd long ago been trained not to think about.

"I . . . I think I have a mom and dad, too," he said slowly. "I remember . . . I remember . . ." his voice then began to trail off.

"You remember what?" Frank asked, urging the boy on. "What do your mother and father look like?"

"I . . . Yes," Omega said faintly. "I can see . . . I can see m-my dad. I'm in a car, a blue car, and . . . he's driving the car, and . . ."

At this point, the boy stopped speaking and snapped out of his trance. Fearing what would happen if they pressed further, Frank and Joe asked him no more questions. But they now had all the information they needed. These youths had not been born in test tubes at all! They had probably been kidnapped as George had been, then brainwashed to forget who they were and where they came from!

"Now listen," Frank addressed the boys firmly. "We know that all of you have parents just like ours. Your master took you away from them and made you forget. But if you help us, we can bring you back to your real parents. I'm sure they miss you terribly."

Frank's last words were like a magic key. The blank looks began to fade from the boys' faces, as if they had been at last released from a deep spell.

"Your names aren't really Omega, Beta, and Alpha," Frank went on. "They're just letters of the Greek alphabet—names your master invented for you when he took away your real ones and destroyed your identities."

Tears welled up in the youngsters' eyes as they remembered the homes they'd been taken from, homes that were now just faint memories.

"By the way, where is your friend, Delta?" Frank asked.

"In the second truck with the others. There

are seven of us all together," Omega whispered.

Frank continued to talk softly and soothingly to the boys until the cloudy veil in their eyes burned off like morning fog and was replaced by a blazing hatred for Rhee and everything he had done to them.

"I'll kill the master!" Omega cried out.

Frank put his finger to his lips. "Shhhh. . . . Don't worry," he whispered. "We'll get you all home, and your master will pay for what he's—"

He stopped in mid-sentence as Candir Karu jumped to his feet and hurried toward the boys.

"What are you kids talking about!" he demanded. "Did I hear one of you say something about killing the master?"

Omega began to move toward Karu, but Joe frantically motioned for him to stop before the foreign agent noticed. Omega got the message. He sat down again, assuming the blank look that was expected of him.

"No," Frank explained quickly. "But he got angry because I asked them to kill the master."

Playing along, Omega nodded fiercely. "I said I would *never* kill the master. And if the master didn't need these two for his work, I'd bust 'em up right now!"

A smile crept over Karu's face. "Nice try," he

178

said, grabbing Frank and Joe by their shirts and dragging them away from the group of boys. "But I think you've done enough visiting. You've only made things worse for yourselves."

With that, he lugged Frank and Joe back to the far end of the truck's cargo hold.

The canvas-covered truck bounced along in the pitch-black night, giving the Hardys enough time to think up a scheme. Finally they arrived at the banks of a river near a wooden dock and the rear door was opened. Frank and Joe noticed a fishing boat at the end of the pier.

"It isn't the same one Karu used before," Joe observed, seeing that the craft was longer and sleeker.

"They aren't taking any more chances," Frank muttered in disgust.

While the gear was being carried to the boat, the Hardys were tied to a tree and guarded by one of the lumberjacks. They saw the second truck, which had been driven by Lafoote. He and Rhee were now busily overseeing the transfer of gear to the fishing boat. Candir Karu, however, had gone right from the truck to the boat to await their departure.

"We can take over for you," a youthful voice hailed the lumberjack who guarded the Hardys.

"They need you to help with the heavy equipment."

The logger nodded and left, and Omega approached the tree where the brothers were tied up. Alpha and Beta were close behind.

"How come you didn't want me to fight with Karu in the truck?" Omega whispered. "We could have escaped out the back of it right then."

Frank shook his head. "Karu carries a knife, and he knows how to use it. Anyway, even if we'd escaped, we would've lost both Lafoote and your master, whose real name, by the way, is Randolph Rhee."

"So we'll untie you now," the boy said. "We know what kind of boat they're on. We can all just run off into the forest and keep going until we find a phone to call the police."

Frank smiled, happy to see that beneath the blank-faced zombie of just a short time ago there was a bright, quick-thinking, normal boy. "I doubt we'll find a phone by morning, and by then Mr. Rhee will be long gone," he warned.

"So think of something better!" Omega urged. "And hurry!"

"Okay. It's a bit risky, but we may be able to capture the whole gang and save the other boys." Quickly Frank outlined his strategy.

Omega huddled with Alpha and Beta for a moment, then turned back to the Hardys.

"We'll do it," he said. "But I sure hope your plan works!"

19 A Confession

When the lumberjacks were ready to load Frank and Joe onto the boat, Omega and his two companions had already climbed aboard and were preparing to carry out Frank's instructions.

"Okay, in you go," the men said and carried the young detectives on board like two sacks of potatoes. Frank and Joe had only a few moments to size up the situation. There were over twenty people on the craft: six lumberjacks, including Lafoote, seven brainwashed boys, Candir Karu, Randolph Rhee, and four or five crewmen. The boat, called *Sea Dancer,* was sixty feet long, big enough to handle an ocean passage without difficulty. It was an old tuna fishing vessel built for spending weeks at sea.

"What'll we do with them, boss?" one of the lumberjacks asked, pointing to the Hardys.

"Put them down in my cabin," Rhee barked. "And make sure they're tied up nice and tight. These kids are as slippery as wet logs!"

A moment later, Frank and Joe were unceremoniously dumped on the floor of a small sleeper cabin under the bow. Once the tuna boat was well under way down the river, Rhee walked in.

"Hello, boys," he greeted them. "Thought I'd come in and get to know you a bit better. I didn't have much time before, since I was so busy with the move."

Joe glared at the scientist. "Why the interest in getting to know us?" he queried coldly. "I thought we were just a couple of new guinea pigs for your experiments."

"Don't think of it that way," Rhee answered brightly. "Think of me as your . . . well . . . your new father. I take good care of my boys, and you'll be very happy once you get adjusted to our little family."

"You mean like those other boys you kidnapped and turned into walking zombies?" Frank snapped.

Rhee sat down on a crate and folded his hands behind his head. "Yes. They were all as upset as you at first about having to leave their homes. But after a few weeks, with the help of a technique I've perfected, they had no memory at all of their real parents and their childhoods. They're all quite happy now with their new lives."

"That's what *you* think!" Joe wanted to retort, but he kept quiet.

"So you're planning to brainwash us, too, is that it?" Frank asked.

Rhee's grin widened. "When we arrive in Greenland and have some time to set things up, I'll put you through my program. Why, in a short time, you won't even know your real names anymore!"

Again the Hardys felt chills run down their spines, imagining themselves transformed into zombies for the rest of their lives. If their plan failed, or if Omega had a change of heart, it would happen!

"You're crazy!" Frank cried out.

The scientist shrugged. "Perhaps I am," he said, feeling the need to defend himself. "But I'm really not such a bad sort. I don't know what you've heard about me, but I used to be a respected leader in the field of genetic engineering. Then, for some stupid reason, the United States government decided to cut off my funds, just when I was on the verge of a major breakthrough!"

Frank and Joe sensed that they were about to hear a full confession. Criminals often did that to show off in front of their victims.

"We heard about the NIH project," Joe said dryly. "We also know that the government abandoned the project for a good reason."

"It was a stupid reason!" the scientist cried angrily. Then he calmed down again, a faraway look in his eyes. "Many times in history, people have stood in the path of science, afraid of where it might take them, afraid of the unknown. I am just one of many great men in history who have had to carry on their work against the government's wishes. You may remember that Galileo, the famous Italian astronomer and physicist, was thrown in jail because he proved Copernicus' theory that the earth was *not* the center of the universe. And there was Leonardo da Vinci, the great Florentine artist and engineer, who had to steal corpses from the morgue in order to study the human anatomy. These great men—fathers of modern science and medicine—were scorned in their time by ignorant governments. They were like me, bravely—"

"Galileo and da Vinci didn't kidnap children for their experiments," Frank interrupted the man's ramblings.

"They did not face the same problems that I do," Rhee shot back, undeterred by the remark. "At first, I only wished to be left alone to carry on my work. I moved to Canada with what little equipment and money I had. For two years I worked alone. But then I required more equipment, more money, and I needed live subjects on which to test my theories. Without that, my work would mean nothing."

"So what did you do then?" Joe probed.

"To get the money, I contacted a foreign country that I knew was looking for ways to produce better athletes for the Olympics. I told them I could genetically engineer such people for them if they funded me. They agreed."

"That's where Mr. Karu fits in," Frank deduced.

"He's their agent. He came to Canada now and then to bring money and make sure that my work was bearing fruit, so to speak. He believes I'm actually on my way to producing superathletes."

"And are you?" Joe asked.

Randolph Rhee shook his head. "I have made a few important discoveries, but I'm still a long way from applying them successfully. You see, Karu and his country think these kids of mine are the results of my work. That's why Karu still gives me support. He doesn't know that my boys were simply kidnapped from very tall, athletic parents rather than produced in my own lab. That's part of the reason I've brainwashed them, named them after Greek letters, and taught them to call me their master. It makes Karu think they were all manufactured from test tubes."

"But why do you want to keep *us*?" Joe argued. "Karu knows you didn't genetically produce us."

"Because you two have it up here." Rhee grinned, pointing to his head. "The other kids are big and strong, but it also takes agility, cunning, wits, and intelligence to produce the superhuman I'm looking for. That's why I'm so glad to have you Hardys aboard, so I can study your genetic makeup. I've heard that your father is a famous investigator and it is clear that you have the same talent. This means that to some extent, your ability is inherited. By studying your chromosomes, I will learn which genes make you such good detectives, then I will

187

splice together your genes with those of great athletes—and *voilà*, a superboy!"

"I guess you'll need someone like George Watley from Camp Ketchumken to complete your formula," Frank prodded. "Do you have another one in mind?"

"Unfortunately, no." The scientist shrugged. "It took a lot of work to set up the Watley kidnapping. But two of my boys are almost as good as George would have been. I will have to use them."

"What about the Paul Bunyan, Junior story? Did you initiate that?"

"That was Lafoote's idea," Rhee admitted. "He knew how superstitious the lumberjacks around here were about Bunyan, so he invented the tale about Bunyan's giant offspring to scare them. You see, from the money the foreign country gave me, I hired Lafoote to abduct the boys and be my protector. He spread the Bunyan myth to force other lumberjacks to help him and keep their mouths shut, and I payed him well for the service. He also built a pair of giant boots to make footprints around our camp, and he made the big ax you saw leaning against the barn door. The few men who dared come to the mountains to see for themselves if the Bunyan family lived there ran back to their camps and confirmed Lafoote's story. That way, nobody gave me any trouble."

"He must have done quite a job on that weird cult in Vermont. They think you're the Devil himself. Did you frame them for George's kidnapping?" Frank asked.

"My, my." Rhee chuckled smugly. "I have a bigger reputation than I imagined. But I've never quite thought of myself as the Devil. That must be a spinoff from the Bunyan legend we circulated. There's no limit to rumors once they get started, is there?"

"There certainly isn't," Joe muttered in disgust.

"Aren't you afraid we'll tell Karu about the way you've been tricking him?" Frank asked, nervous over Rhee's intentions. "If he comes down here we'll be able to tell him everything you've said so far."

"No, you won't," the scientist chortled, and withdrew a syringe from his jacket pocket. "In a few more seconds, you'll be sleeping again. And when you wake up, Karu will be long gone and you'll be in Greenland!"

Frank and Joe gulped. If they were unconscious, their plan could not possibly succeed!

"You won't have to do that," Joe assured him. "We won't tell Karu anything. We're smart, remember?"

"Oh, I was going to do it anyway, Karu or not," Rhee said. "I can't take any chances with you two. As I always say, better safe than sorry."

He bent down, preparing to stick the needle in Joe's arm. But as he did, shouts of alarm suddenly erupted from the deck above.

"Fire! Fire!"

The Hardys gasped with relief as Rhee tucked the syringe back in his pocket and ran out of the cabin. A moment later, the door flung open again and Omega rushed in.

"You're just in time," Joe breathed.

The boy nodded and speedily untied the young detectives' ropes. Then he raced to the bridge ahead of them, telling the skipper that he was needed on the foredeck. At first the captain was reluctant to leave his post, but when he finally did, Frank rushed up and flipped the switch on the ship-to-shore radio.

He contacted the marine operator and asked her to place a call to Halifax, while Joe went to search for the engine compartment. Everyone else was busy helping to squelch a blazing fire that Alpha and Beta had started with old, oily

191

rags and cardboard boxes. Frank would have the bridge to himself for a few moments, but it would not be long before the fire was out.

"Hello?" the CIA agent's voice crackled thinly over the radio receiver.

"Mr. Chester, this is Frank Hardy. SOS. Get as many men together as you can and go to the mouth of the St. John River. Do you read?"

"Frank? Where are you? I've had my men out looking for you for two—"

Frank had glanced through the window. Already the fire was nearly out and the men were beginning to turn away. "I have no time to explain," he interrupted the federal agent. "We're on a sixty-foot tuna boat named *Sea Dancer* with Rhee and about twenty others. Be at the reversing falls as soon as possible. Prepare to intercept us. Over and out."

He switched off the radio, then left the bridge before he was spotted and ran back to the sleeper cabin. Joe was already there, wiping his greasy hands on a blanket.

"Did you get him?" the blond boy asked anxiously.

"Yes. What about you?"

"I found a water intake valve for the engine and loosened it up. It ought to give out in a few more minutes."

"Good. Let's hope for some miracles."

Omega came into the cabin and quickly bound the sleuths' ankles and wrists again. He had gone by the time Rhee appeared at the door.

"Now, where were we when I was so rudely interrupted?" The scientist grinned wickedly.

Without waiting for a reply, he stuck a needle in Joe's arm. Then he sedated Frank. The brothers were once again helplessly drifting off into unconsciousness.

20 Caught!

"I think they're coming around," a distant voice penetrated Frank's clouded mind as he slowly began to wake up.

He felt a cool, wet sensation on his forehead as his thoughts cleared and he remembered Randolph Rhee standing over him, hypodermic needle in hand. At first, Frank didn't dare open his eyes, afraid of where he might be. It wasn't until he heard the voice a second time that a wide smile broke over his face and his eyes flickered open.

"Chet," he said weakly. "Chet, old boy, am I ever glad to see you. I thought I was in Greenland!"

"I'm glad you're glad." Chet Morton smiled as he dabbed Frank's forehead with a wet cloth. "You've been out cold for almost twenty-four hours."

Gazing about, Frank saw that he was in a bedroom in the Hooper summer cottage in Vermont. With him were Chet, Biff, Mr. Hooper, Lieutenant Henderson, and Fenton Hardy. Joe was still unconscious on a cot next to his.

"I feel like I just woke up from a nightmare," Frank said, then focused on his father. "I guess our plan worked, huh, Dad?"

"We surrounded the tuna boat at the mouth of the St. John River." Mr. Hardy beamed proudly. "It had just missed getting through the reversing falls, so it was a sitting duck. Rhee and his gang are on their way to jail on ten counts of kidnapping."

"What about the boys?" Frank asked worriedly. He was a little fuzzy as he swung his legs to the floor and sat up.

"Rhee kept records of their real parents. Once they're through an orientation program to wipe out the effects of the brainwashing, they'll be taken back to their homes."

Joe began to stir on his cot, and raised himself on an elbow.

"How did we get here?" he murmured.

195

"After we rescued you from the boat, Mr. Chester suggested you finish the vacation you started," his father replied. "He'll want to ask you some questions later, but for now, he said, you were due a rest. So we put you on a government jet and flew you back here."

"Need a rest?" Joe laughed. "I've been resting for so long I feel like Rip Van Winkle! I'll tell you what I need—a good meal! I'm starved!"

"Same here," Frank agreed, realizing that they hadn't had anything to eat since the cheese and apples they'd taken from the lumber camp.

"I'm pretty hungry myself," Chet admitted, patting his plump stomach. "I've been so concerned about you two, I forgot to have breakfast."

"I find that hard to believe," Joe kidded.

In jubilant spirits, the boys led the group down to the kitchen, where they fixed a feast of bacon and eggs. Soon, Frank and Joe began to feel like their old selves again and up to going over the details of the case.

"Rhee told us everything except how he set up George's kidnapping," Joe said after repeating the scientist's account of events.

"I got that from Smith," Lieutenant Henderson spoke up. "I turns out that Smith and Lafoote used to work together as lumberjacks and were old buddies. When Smith found himself in desperate financial straits, he asked Lafoote to help him out. Lafoote made him an offer. If Smith could get the son of a famous athlete to come to his camp and then send him off by himself, Lafoote would bail the camp director out of his financial trouble. The camp would've gone under anyway, so Smith didn't care that the scandal might shut it down—as long as he had enough money for himself."

"Did he know what was going to happen to George?" Frank asked.

"No. He thought the boy would be held for ransom and was assured that George would not be harmed."

"Rhee actually went to Boston himself to check out George and make sure the boy would be a good subject," Mr. Hardy put in. "George lives with his parents in a townhouse near the football stadium, and Rhee spied on him for several days."

"Rhee must've been returning from that trip when Jeffrey Peters, his old partner in the NIH research team, ran into him on the train," Joe said. Then he told Chet and Biff the story of their Canadian adventure, starting with their train ride and ending with how they'd set the tuna boat up for capture.

"Wow! That part about you guys in the saw-mill gives me the jitters!" Chet exclaimed, wide-eyed.

Frank grinned. "I'll tell you this—I don't want to see any firewood for a long, long time."

"Hey!" Joe blurted in mock indignation, suddenly remembering that their chunky friend had a score of his own to settle. "Frank and I caught *our* fish! But what about your wayward bass? You told us you'd have Old Sam hung on the wall in less than a week."

Chet's face flushed. "I . . . er, haven't quite snared him yet," he said defensively. "But I *know* he's down there because he's already bitten off three of my lines. Took the whole thing each time, hooks and all. But now I have a seventy-pound line and I'll be bringing him in today, for sure."

Joe rolled his eyes. "I bet your bites turn out to be just an old log in the bottom of the lake."

"Logs don't swim around in circles under your boat," Chet protested.

"Maybe it's the boat that was going around in circles!" The blond boy laughed. "Yup, I bet Old Sam is just a big old sycamore!"

"Why don't we go with you as witnesses?" Frank suggested. "If we don't get him today, then he obviously doesn't exist. Is it a deal, Chet?"

The plump youth smirked. "Okay, okay. It's a deal."

The young detectives said good-bye to Mr. Hardy and Lt. Henderson, who still had a lot of paperwork to go over with the local police and the CIA. Biff and his father offered to take temporary charge of Camp Ketchumken, and soon left to look after the boys. Frank, Joe, and Chet then headed for the lake.

"Here we go!" Joe shouted gleefully, throttling up the green skiff's powerful outboard. "Watch out, Old Sam. We're wise to you now!"

The boat skimmed over the beautiful, clear Vermont lake until it reached the north end.

"Cut it!" Chet ordered. "This is the spot."

Joe shut off the outboard and soon all three boys had their hooks baited and in the water.

"Now hold your rods tight," Chet instructed. "Like I said, this is a seventy-pound test line. If Old Sam grabs it and you're not paying attention, he'll yank you right out of the boat and you'll be flyin' with the crows."

"Aye-aye, captain." Frank grinned.

"Relax," Joe quipped, holding his rod casually in one hand while munching on a pear. "There isn't a fish in this whole lake that could—"

Suddenly, his line snapped as taut as a piano wire! An instant later, the fishing rod tore out of his hand and flew over the side of the skiff as if

Paul Bunyan himself were tugging at the hook. Gaping, Joe watched the rod disappear down into the watery depths.

"Whaddaya say now, wise guy?" Chet gloated. "I told you to hang on tight!"

"Well, I'll be . . ." the blond boy murmured in disbelief, scratching his head as he stared transfixed into the blue-green water. "I guess Old Sam is for real after all!"

For the rest of the week, the boys took turns helping out at Camp Ketchumken and spent their spare time on the lake hoping to catch Old Sam. But they never got another nibble from the giant bass. When the three finally had to go back to Bayport, though, they vowed not to give up.

"Biff, it's a great spot your family's got here— and you've been terrific hosts," Joe said in thanks.

"You guys are easy houseguests—you're hardly ever around!" Biff responded good-naturedly. "I bet you'll be working on a new case in no time!"

His prediction came true when the Hardys found themselves involved with *The Blackwing Puzzle*.

Coming soon . . .
from Archway Paperbacks

THE HARDY BOYS®
CASE FILES
by Franklin W. Dixon

HAVE YOU SEEN THE HARDY BOYS LATELY?
Bond has high-tech equipment, Indiana Jones
courage and daring . . .
ONLY THE HARDY BOYS HAVE IT ALL!!

Now you can continue to enjoy the Hardy Boys in a new
action-packed series written especially for older readers.
Each pocket-sized paperback has more high-tech adventure,
intrigue, mystery and danger than ever before.

In the new Hardy Boys Case Files, Frank and Joe pursue one
thrilling adventure after another. With their intelligence,
charm, knowledge of the martial arts and their state-of-the-art
equipment, the Hardys find themselves investigating international terrorism, espionage rings, religious cults, and crime
families. Whether they're in Europe or Bayport, The Hardy
Boys® are never far from life-or-death action.

#1 DEAD ON TARGET
The sudden death by bombing of Joe's girlfriend, Iola, pro-
pels the Hardy Boys into a hunt for a band of international
terrorists who have targeted a presidential candidate for a
bloodbath in the Bayport Mall. But Frank and Joe will have to
combat the terrorists' leader, the infamous Al-Rousasa (Ara-
bic for "The Bullet"). Al-Rousasa is as good as his name.
When he shoots, he shoots to kill.

Read on . . .

#2 CULT OF CRIME

The Hardys jet off on an all-expense paid trip to Paris, where their assignment is to investigate Paul Reynard, a French businessman who may just be the head of an international crime empire. Frank and Joe go undercover in Paris posing as punked-out drifters in search of illegal weapons. As soon as they arrive they are plunged into a nightmarish train of events, in which they are arrested, imprisoned, and framed as cop-killers. If they reveal their identities, they will blow their cover and alert Reynard. So they flee to Normandy, where, unknown to them the Reynard family has learned their mission and waits to execute them.

#3 EVIL, INC.

The Hardys set out to find Holly, a young girl who has fallen into the clutches of a California cult. The cult's background may be religious, but the motivation is pure crime. Frank and Joe manage to rescue Holly, but must flee cross country with both the police and angry cult members on their trail. What the Hardys don't realize is that Holly has been completely brainwashed. One word from the cult leader could set her off on a path of destruction so terrible that it could leave the town of Bayport in a state of total ruin.

Look for THE HARDY BOYS CASE FILES novels at your local bookstore!

**Archway Paperbacks
Published by Pocket Books**

131